D0542636

A Death in Indian Wells

OTHER SAGEBRUSH LARGE PRINT WESTERNS BY
LEWIS B. PATTEN

Apache Hostage
No God In Saguaro
Two for Vengeance

A Death in Indian Wells

LEWIS B. PATTEN

Sagebrush
Large Print Westerns

Library of Congress Cataloging-in-Publication Data

Patten, Lewis B.
  A death in Indian Wells / Lewis B. Patten
      p.   cm.
  ISBN 1-57490-479-5 (lg. print : hardcover)
 1. Cheyenne Indians—Fiction. 2. Sheriffs—Fiction. 3.
Lynching—Fiction. 4. Large type books. I. Title.

PS3566.A79D39 2003
813'.54—dc21   2003005099

Cataloging in Publication Data is available from
the British Library and the National Library of Australia.

LINCOLNSHIRE
COUNTY COUNCIL

Copyright © 1970 by Lewis. B. Patten. Published by
arrangement with Golden West Literary Agency. All rights
reserved.

Sagebrush Large Print Westerns are published in the
United States and Canada by Thomas T. Beeler, Publisher, PO
Box 659, Hampton Falls, New Hampshire 03844-0659. ISBN 1-
57490-479-5

Published in the United Kingdom, Eire, and the Republic of
South Africa by Isis Publishing Ltd, 7 Centremead, Osney
Mead, Oxford OX2 0ES England. ISBN 0-7531-6914-2

Published in Australia and New Zealand by Bolinda Publishing
Pty Ltd, 17 Mohr Street, Tullamarine, Victoria, Australia, 3043
ISBN 1-74030-921-9

Manufactured by Sheridan Books in Chelsea, Michigan.

A Death in Indian Wells

CHAPTER 1

THERE WERE THREE OF THEM, AT FIRST ONLY SPECKS on the tawny, rolling plain, then horses with riders, in single file the way the Indians ride.

Pete Handy, grizzled and weathered by his fifty-five years, much of which had been spent in the mountains and on this empty plain, rode in the lead, slouched comfortably, seeming to doze but missing nothing either on the land or in the sky. Behind him rode the prisoner, hands cuffed in front of him. Behind the prisoner came Joseph, Handy's nineteen-year-old son. Joseph was no darker of skin than his father, yet there was a difference immediately apparent to anyone. Joseph was half Indian.

Pete Handy wore a tarnished silver sheriff's star. Joseph wore an equally tarnished deputy's badge made of bronze. Their prisoner had shot an unarmed man in the course of a fight in the Free State Saloon and had fled west immediately afterward, three days ago. Handy and Joseph had caught up with him the second day and had captured him without firing a shot. Now they were returning him to Indian Wells for trial.

At midday, the sun was hot, but earlier there had been a coolness in the air, a chill and frosty smell, as if winter was gathering over the spine of Rocky Mountains three hundred miles farther west. It was mid-October and the year was 1872.

Indian Wells lay in a valley below a marshy flat out of which the three springs rose that had given the town its name. The flow from the three joined and ran down the valley, a trickle that supplied the town with water

1

and went by the name of Indian Creek.

The town's earlier buildings had been built of prairie sod. Still standing, some of them were still in use for storage purposes. The later buildings were of frame construction, some painted white, some of rough-sawed lumber turned gray with weathering and age.

There were a hundred and seventeen permanent residents in Indian Wells. There were usually a few buffalo hunters in town for supplies and on Saturday nights maybe a dozen cowhands from ranches in the surrounding area.

On the south side of town was Sol Radinski's hide yard, a fenced half-acre where board-stiff buffalo hides were piled awaiting shipment by freight wagon to the railroad at Dodge. Wherever the wind blew out of the south, everyone in town held their noses and wondered why somebody didn't do something about that smell. But the hide yard brought the buffalo hunters to Indian Wells and with them a certain amount of prosperity. So nobody did anything but complain.

The hoofs of the three horses stirred the dust on Main Street and the breeze lifted it and carried it away. There was a crowd in front of the Indian Wells Hardware Store, staring through the large glass show window that had been installed a year ago, having been freighted all the way from St. Louis in a crate.

The heads of those in front of the hardware store turned toward the horsemen coming down the street. Pete Handy spoke to his son. "I wonder what the hell's so interesting in the hardware store."

Joseph shrugged. Luke Kitchen, the prisoner, was white-faced now and scared. He'd been drunk the night of the fight. Getting the worst of it, he'd pulled his gun and fired without even thinking about whether the other

2

man was armed or not. He hadn't intended to commit murder but he had and now it was time to pay the price.

In front of the hardware store, Pete Handy drew his horse to a sudden halt. Looking over the heads of those gathered there, he could see through the window, could see the enclosed area beyond it where Silas Grosbeck usually displayed guns and other merchandise. Today it held a different kind of display, one that made a flush rise into Handy's weathered face. He heeled his horse up across the boardwalk and forced the spectators to move aside by the simple expedient of riding into them.

There was an Indian in the window, a young Indian brave, naked except for breechclout and moccasins. He wore a single feather in his braided hair. He was conscious but he was wounded and he had lost a lot of blood. There was a pool of it on the floor. He had a bloody wound in his right thigh. There was another bullet hole in the left side of his chest from which a light pink froth bubbled every time he breathed.

His eyes, dark and impassive, met Handy's glance steadily. A chain secured his ankles to a steel ringbolt in the floor. Manacles secured his wrists and another chain connected his wrists to the ankle chain. The manacles had apparently been forged by a blacksmith, and carelessly because there were burns on both of the Indian's wrists and on his ankles.

The Indian was no older than Handy's son, and suddenly the sheriff's sense of outrage flared. He turned his head and glared with cold anger at the spectators. "Just who the hell is responsible for this?"

No one answered him. None of them would look at him. Several hurried away. A couple turned their heads to stare at Joseph with smoldering dislike.

Handy swung from his horse. He was used to seeing

3

Joseph looked at that way. He looped the reins around the rail and glanced up at his son. "Take Kitchen down and lock him up. Then get a wagon at the livery barn and bring it here."

Joseph rode away toward the jail, with Kitchen following. There had been a certain impassive quality about Joseph's expression but it hadn't fooled his father. Handy knew his son was just as furious as he was.

He went into the hardware store and roared, "Silas!" Grosbeck came hurrying down the aisle from his office in the rear. He was a squat, muscular man, pale from working indoors. He wore a neatly trimmed beard and a leather apron.

Handy asked angrily, "Is that your idea?"

"The Injun? Huh uh. Three buffalo hunters brought him in. They asked me if I'd let them keep him in there and I said I would. I figured it would be good for business. Has been too. There's been people in front of that window ever since they put him there."

"He's hurt. Didn't it occur to anybody to get Doc Bennett to look at him?"

"Hell, he's only an Injun, Pete." Grosbeck remembered suddenly that Pete Handy's son was half Indian. "I don't . . . didn't mean . . . Well hell, you know what I mean."

"Yeah. I think I do know what you mean. Now I'm going to tell you what I mean. If that Indian dies, you're an accessory to his murder. So get your ass over to Doc's and tell him to come down to the jail right away."

"You can't talk to me like that."

The flush suddenly left Pete Handy's face. His coldly angry eyes held those of Grosbeck and the color drained quickly out of Grosbeck's face. He mumbled, "All right. All right. No call to get so goddam mad." He turned and

4

hurried out the front door into the sun-washed, dusty street.

Pete Handy stepped to the waist-high partition leading to the display area. He looked over it at the young Indian. He spoke softly in the Cheyenne tongue. "I am sorry for what has been done to you. I will have you out of there soon. The medicine man will look at your wounds. Have you had anything to eat?"

The Cheyenne turned his head. He stared at Handy but he didn't speak. There was implacable hatred in his eyes. Handy shrugged. "Can't blame you for hating me," he said in English. He studied the Indian's face, seeing now the flush of fever, the weakness that was in the man.

He got a hacksaw from Grosbeck's shelf and began to saw through the ringbolt in the floor. He heard a wagon creak to a halt out front. Joseph came in. Pete finished cutting the bolt and opened the gate in the low partition. Joseph stepped up into the store window display area. Handy lifted the Indian's upper body, Joseph his legs. They carried him out chains clanking, and placed him in the wagon. Joseph climbed to the seat. Handy untied and mounted his horse and rode along behind. The townspeople in the street stared after them.

At the stone block jail, Joseph pulled the wagon to a halt. Handy tied his horse to the rail in front. He unlocked the door, went in and opened the barred door leading to the cells. Luke Kitchen was sitting despondently on a bench in the first cell on the right. Handy opened the one across from it, then went back outside.

He and Joseph carried the Indian in and laid him carefully on the bunk inside the cell. The man still had not lost consciousness although it was apparent that he

5

was in great pain. His bronzed skin had a grayish pallor to it and sweat had drenched his forehead and upper lip. Joseph stayed in the cell and as Handy went back through the office into the street, he could hear Joseph talking to the wounded Indian in the Cheyenne tongue. The man did not reply.

Staring up the baking, dusty street, Handy saw Grosbeck returning. He untied his horse, mounted and trotted the animal up the street. He reached Grosbeck's store just as Grosbeck did, and looked down at him questioningly. "Well? Where is he?"

"Doc? He said to tell you not to call on him to treat any damn Indians. He said he was here back in '67 when the Cheyenne were butchering settlers like they were sheep."

Handy opened his mouth to tell Grosbeck that Chivington had started it all at Sand Creek in '64 but he closed it again without saying anything. Words wouldn't calm the hatred that existed between Indian and white. He nodded curtly and Grosbeck went into the store after a resentful glance at the sheriff's office.

Handy looked down at the jail, then up the street toward Doc Bennett's house. He hesitated only a moment before riding up the street.

He dismounted in front of Doc's house, a two-story, white frame with a picket fence around a small plot of browning grass. There was a sign on the door reading W. J. BENNETT, M.D.

Handy tied his horse to the iron hitching post and went up the walk. He twisted the bell and waited impatiently. Doc Bennett came to the door and scowled at the sheriff. Handy said, "I sent Grosbeck after you. There's a wounded Indian down at the jail and you're the only doctor in a hundred miles."

6

Bennett was a tall, gaunt man. His hair was untidily long and he wore a drooping mustache but no beard. He wore a vest over his rumpled shirt and his sleeves were secured by elastic above the elbows. He said irritably, "I told Grosbeck I didn't intend to treat any Indians."

"What kind of a doctor are you for Christ's sake? He's shot twice and if he doesn't get help he's going to die."

"What kind of doctor am I? I'll tell you, Sheriff. I'm the kind of doctor that has treated a woman driven insane by being raped repeatedly by all the members of a war party that killed and scalped her husband right before her eyes. I'm the kind of doctor that has helped bury murdered children and bodies that the Indians had mutilated until it was damn hard to tell who they were. Don't you stand there with that holier-than-thou look on your face and ask me what kind of doctor I am. I'm a doctor that treats human beings, not animals. You go find a vet to treat your Indian."

"You know there isn't a vet in Indian Wells." Handy stared at the doctor. The hell of it was, he could see both sides of this. Bennett started to close the door but Handy stuck his foot in it. "Doc, I'm not asking you, I'm telling you. Get your bag and come down to the jail. If you refuse to treat him, I'm going to arrest you and throw you in the cell next to him."

Bennett stared at him unbelievingly. "You're what? On what charge, for God's sake?"

"Accessory to murder. Because if you don't treat him, that Indian is going to die."

"You'll never make it stick. No jury in Kansas . . ."

Handy said softly, "Maybe not, Doc, but I can keep you in jail until the circuit judge gets here two weeks from now."

7

Bennett stared closely at Handy's face for a time. He was scowling but there was a grudging respect in him. At last he shrugged, turned, and came back a moment later with his hat and coat and his scarred leather bag. He came out onto the porch, handed the sheriff his bag and shrugged into his coat. As he reached for the bag again he asked, "How do you know I won't kill him instead of trying to make him well?"

"I'll take the chance."

Resignedly Bennett followed Handy down the walk to where his horse was tied. Again he handed the sheriff his bag while he mounted the sheriff's horse. Handy mounted behind him, after passing up the bag. Riding double, the two trotted down the street toward the jail.

Grosbeck was standing in the doorway of his hardware store. He scowled steadily at Handy as he and the doctor passed.

Reaching the jail, the sheriff dismounted and held the horse while Doc Bennett swung stiffly down. He tied the horse, then led the way into the jail.

Joseph came out of the wounded Indian's cell. Doc Bennett went in and put his bag on the floor beside the cot. He pulled the bench close, sat down, removed his spectacles from his vest pocket and put them on.

The wounded Indian exploded into action suddenly and unexpectedly. He flung himself at Doc, toppling his bench and knocking him sprawling. Doc's glasses fell off his nose and one lens shattered on the floor.

Handy and Joseph immediately rushed into the cell. They reached the Indian and subdued him before he could do more. They put him back on the bunk. Handy sat down, holding the chain that secured the Indian's wrists. Joseph held his ankle chains.

Doc Bennett got to his feet, cursing angrily. He

scowled at the Indian, whose dark, hate-filled eyes glared implacably back at him. Surprisingly he said, "Hell, he ain't hardly more than a boy."

He stooped and retrieved his broken glasses, grumbling. He picked the broken glass carefully out of the gold frame, then put the spectacles back on. "Maybe I can get by with just one lens."

Handy said, "We'll hold him, Doc. Go ahead and do what you can for him."

Doc replaced the bench beside the cot. He put his bag on the bench beside him and opened it. Frowning now at the seriousness of the chest wound, he went to work.

CHAPTER 2

SWEATING HEAVILY, PETE HANDY FOLLOWED DOC Bennett out into the street. He had watched, holding the struggling Indian, while Bennett probed for and found the bullet lodged in the Indian's thigh. The young brave had fainted as Doc began probing for the bullet in his chest and Bennett had given up, grunting, "I'll kill him if I keep this up. He needs some rest. Maybe tomorrow or the next day if he's still alive, I can get that slug."

Now the Indian lay bandaged and unconscious on the narrow cot. Joseph sat with him, watching his face, feeling, Handy knew, a kind of kinship he had never felt for any white. Doc Bennett walked up the street, carrying his scuffed black leather bag.

Pete Handy stared after him. In midafternoon, only a few people were visible. He knew them all but he wasn't paying any attention to them. He was thinking back, remembering a lot of things that had happened a long time ago.

He'd known the mountain men, and had trapped beaver with them in the early days. Bridger, StVrain, Vasquez, Uncle Dick Wootton, the Bents. In '54 he fell in love with a Cheyenne girl and married her according to Cheyenne law. Joseph was born a year afterward.

A faint smile touched his mouth and his eyes were far away from this place, far from this time. They'd had ten happy years. But Chivington's slaughter of the Cheyenne at Sand Creek in '64 had forced him to make a choice—to choose between remaining with the Cheyenne and permitting Joseph to grow up already doomed, or returning to the whites. He chose the latter course.

Bird Woman came with him; bringing Joseph, who then was nine. They went to Denver and Handy took a job driving a freight wagon to the mines.

Bird Woman, who had been laughing and happy in the Indian village now became silent and serious and her eyes turned sad. She spoke English well, having learned from Pete, but none of the Denver women would talk to her. She was a squaw, a hated Indian, and they would have nothing to do with her. She became thin and frail, and at last Handy admitted to himself that she would die if he did not take her back.

So he took her back and for a short time they lived with the Indians again, until he realized that if he remained, Joseph would live out his years as an Indian and die on a reservation or in chains.

His eyes, staring unseeingly at the sun-drenched street of Indian Wells, now narrowed with another memory. Parting from Bird Woman had been one of the most painful things he had ever done.

He hadn't seen her now for months. He had hoped that Luke Kitchen's flight would take him north to the

10

area where Bird Woman's people lived, but Kitchen had gone the other way. Bird Woman was still Handy's wife, for all that he didn't see her more than twice a year. They still loved each other as much as they ever had, perhaps more. He was suddenly very lonely for her.

He heard Joseph close the barred door leading to the cells, softly so that he would not awaken the Indian. He turned his head. Joseph stepped out onto the boardwalk, closing the jail door behind him. He said, "He's going to die, isn't he?"

Pete Handy nodded. "Probably. That's a pretty bad wound in his chest and Doc hasn't got a prayer of getting the bullet out. Besides that, he lost a lot of blood, lying in Grosbeck's store window all that time."

"Did you find out who put him there?"

"Not yet. You stay here and keep an eye on things. I'll try to find out now."

"What are you going to do to them?"

"Depends on whether the Indian dies."

"And if he does?"

Handy met his son's glance unflinchingly. There had been a challenge in Joseph's voice. Handy knew there wasn't a chance of convicting the men who had captured and displayed the Indian, but if the Indian died it would be murder just as surely as if the victim had been white. He said, "I'll arrest them and charge them with killing him."

Joseph nodded. The answer seemed to satisfy him but Handy knew his son was as aware as he of the difficulties of convicting anyone of killing an Indian. The people of western Kansas had suffered too much at the hands of the Cheyenne. Too many settlers had been butchered, too many farmhouses burned, too many women carried off.

11

Handy also knew that Joseph stood at a crossroads because of what was happening here in Indian Wells. Here, in the next few days or weeks would be decided whether Joseph would remain with the whites and be one of them or whether he would return to the doomed Indians and perhaps die with them.

Handy turned uptown in the direction Doc Bennett had gone a few minutes earlier. The Free State Saloon was on the corner of Main and Maple, half a block from the jail. Its swinging doors faced diagonally onto the intersection. Handy pushed them open and went in.

There was the usual scattering of buffalo hunters in the place and there was the usual smell of death emanating from their clothes. Handy walked slowly to the bar.

Tony Gallo bald and skinny, wearing a dirty white apron, looked questioningly at him. Handy said, "Beer," and Gallo drew one and slid it down the bar. He followed and said, "I see you caught Luke Kitchen, Pete. Did he give you any fight?"

Handy shook his head. He drank half the beer without taking the mug from his lips, then wiped his mouth with the broad, hairy back of his powerful hand. He asked bluntly, "Who brought that Indian into town?"

"Why?"

Handy scowled at him. "Don't play games with me. Who brought him into town?"

"Three buffalo hunters. They ain't here right now."

"Names?"

Gallo said resignedly, "Holloman, Farley, and Weigand."

"They still around?"

"Sure. They're probably down at their camp on Indian Creek."

Handy finished the rest of his beer. Again he wiped the foam off his mouth with the back of his hand. He laid a nickel on the bar, turned and went outside.

Joseph was watching him from the jail. Handy crossed the street and walked down to Sol Radinski's Hide Yard. He could feel Joseph's steady glance on his back.

He was angry suddenly, angry because he was expected to solve a problem that wasn't solvable. He couldn't stop whites from hating Indians. He couldn't stop Indians from hating whites. Then his anger cooled. Joseph didn't expect that much from him. Joseph only expected that he do what he knew was right. Joseph expected justice for the wounded Indian but maybe he would be satisfied if his father tried.

He reached the hide yard and pushed open the gate. There was a small building in the middle of the yard where Sol Radinski's office was. Handy pushed open the door and went inside, trying to ignore the cloying smell of death that hung like a fog inside the hide yard fence.

Radinski wore a leather apron and a black skull cap. Handy said, "I'm looking for Holloman, Farley, and Weigand. Did they bring in a load of hides?"

Radinski nodded.

"You paid them yet?"

"Drinking money I gave them. Settled up we ain't."

"Don't settle up with them. I want them in town for a couple of days. I don't want to have to chase after them if that Indian dies."

"I can't . . ."

Handy's glance was cold. "You can and you will. Don't settle up with them until I give you the word. If they don't like that, send them to me."

13

Radinski said, "A mistake you're making. There ain't a jury in Kansas that would convict them three."

Handy said, "We're going to give it a try if the Indian dies." He turned and went out, hurried across the hide yard and out into the street. He thought there must be a million flies in the hide yard. They arose in clouds from the ground and from the piles of hides he passed.

Two buffalo hunters were leaving the Free State Saloon. They turned the corner after a quick look at the jail, and headed for the brushy bed of Indian Creek.

Handy crossed to the jail, a look of satisfaction in his eyes. He wouldn't have to hunt for Holloman, Farley, and Weigand. When they found out he had liberated the Indian and that he was looking for them, they'd come to him. Joseph was sitting at the desk inside the jail. Handy looked at him questioningly. Joseph said, "He's still alive, but he's weakening."

Handy crossed the room and went back to look in through the open door of the Indian's cell. The young man lay on his back. His breathing was labored and noisy. His skin was almost gray. Handy considered going after Doc but decided against it. If there had been anything further Doc could do, he'd have done it before he left. He had done an efficient job of removing the bullet in the Indian's leg and an efficient job of bandaging.

Handy returned to the office. He sat down and packed his pipe. He lighted it and puffed it for several minutes, frowning worriedly.

Joseph was watching him. He said, "You don't have to ram me down their throats any more. I can go back and live with the Indians."

Handy glanced at him. "Is that what you want?"

Joseph shook his head. "I don't know what I want.

14

That's the hell of it."

Out in back, the Indian's breathing was becoming noisier. It came in quick gasps. Luke Kitchen's voice raised to call, "When is the judge due, Sheriff?"

"Around the first of the month."

"And I have to stay in here until then?"

"I guess you do."

Kitchen grumbled something the sheriff didn't hear. Joseph rocked back and forth monotonously in the swivel chair. Watching him, Pete Handy cursed sourly to himself. Why the hell couldn't the people of Cheyenne County and particularly those in Indian Wells, accept Joseph for what he was? Joseph thought like a white man. He talked like a white man and lived like one. Someday he would make them the best damn sheriff they'd ever had. He could track like a full-blooded Indian. He wasn't afraid of anything. But most important of all, he had good judgment. He wasn't inclined to act hastily and regret it afterward.

Glancing out through the window, Handy saw five men round the corner of Maple and Main. Two went into the Free State Saloon. The other three continued toward the jail.

He said, "Here they come."

Joseph got up and walked to the window. He stared at the three buffalo hunters coming down the walk abreast. All three carried rifles, the big Sharps buffalo guns they used in their work. In addition, all three had revolvers in holsters at their sides, and knives in scabbards belted higher on the opposite side.

Handy thought wryly that there never was any doubt about what a buffalo hunter's calling was. They smelled alike, for one thing, of dead buffalo, and campfire smoke, and rancid grease, and tobacco and sweat and

15

whisky. Most of them could be smelled a hundred yards away if the wind was right.

And they dressed pretty much alike. Floppy, broad-brimmed hats, shiny with sweat and grease and dust, ragged, faded and dirty shirts and pants. Heavy, flat-heeled boots, covered with blood and grease and manure. Heavy, short coats that a man could work in and still stay warm.

Mostly, too, they wore beards because it was too much trouble trying to shave out on the plains.

The three approaching the jail were typical. The one in the middle was big, over six feet tall. He must weigh, Handy guessed, around two hundred and twenty pounds. His beard was black, heavily tinged with gray. His eyes, blue and close-set and small, were as mean as the eyes of a boar.

Handy fixed his eyes on this one, evaluating him because he knew this was the one with whom he would have to deal.

The door slammed open and the big man came in. The other two followed and instantly the rancid smell of them filled the room. Handy wrinkled his nose deliberately and saw the angry flush creep into the big man's face. Scowling, the man said, "I understan' you got some of our property. We'll take it back now if it's all the same to you."

Handy asked, "Who are you?"

"Sime Holloman." The big man turned his head and spoke to the other two. "He's back there in one of them cells. Get him."

The two started past him toward the cells. Handy's voice cut through the air like a whip. "Don't go back there!"

The two stopped. Holloman said softly, "I said get

16

him out."

For an instant the silence in the room was complete. The only sounds were those made by the breathing of the men and the rasping sounds coming from the dying Indian. Suddenly those sounds stopped.

Handy said, "Go look at him, Joseph. I think he's dead."

Joseph moved past the three men and went into the Indian's cell. He came back in a moment, his dark eyes noticeably expressionless. He nodded at his father, then shifted his glance to Holloman.

Holloman looked closely at Joseph, then at Pete. "Dead you say? Well hell, we don't want him if he's dead."

Handy said, "But I want you."

CHAPTER 3

ONCE MORE SILENCE HUNG LIKE A FOG IN THE TINY room. Holloman stared closely at the sheriff and at his deputy, weighing their potential danger to himself and his two companions. Behind him, the others edged cautiously to left and right. All three seemed to realize suddenly how the rifles in their right hands would handicap them in case this came to a fight.

Holloman started to shift his to his left hand but Handy said sharply, "Leave it where it is!" .

Holloman froze. Neither Handy nor Joseph had drawn gun. Now Handy said, "Reach across with your left hand and pick your pistols out of their holsters. Drop them on the floor."

None of the three complied. The sheriff moved quickly and his gun appeared in his hand. The hammer

17

coming back made a sharp, metallic click. It wasn't necessary for him to repeat his command. Slowly, carefully, the three buffalo hunters reached across, picked the revolvers from their holsters and dropped them, one by one, to the floor. Handy said, "Now the rifles. One at a time."

One by one, the rifles dropped. Handy said, "Get behind them, Joseph, and gather up their guns."

Joseph circled behind his father but he had to go between Holloman and one of the others because of the way the other had edged closer to the wall. As he did, Holloman lunged at him.

Handy fired instantly and saw the bullet whirl Holloman half way around as it tore into his left shoulder. The other man stooped and seized his rifle. As Joseph staggered into him, off balance, he brought it over the young man's head and holding it in both hands, jerked it back against his throat. His knee came up and jammed hard into the small of Joseph's back.

Holloman said, "Drop the gun, Sheriff!" as Joseph choked, desperately trying to draw a breath.

Pete Handy didn't look at Joseph's bulging eyes or at his face. His voice was cold and matter-of-fact. "No. Tell your friend to let him go. I'll kill you if you don't."

Joseph's face was turning blue but Handy still didn't look at him. He had meant what he said and his gun was lined on Holloman's head. His finger tightened almost imperceptibly. His first shot would kill Holloman. His second would bring the third man down. After that he'd be free to go to Joseph's aid.

Holloman's voice came rushing hoarsely out, "Let him go, Farley! God damn it, let him go! This son-of-a-bitch means what he says!"

Farley let go of one end of the rifle. Joseph moved

18

away a step. He turned, gagging and choking. He swung a short, hard left that sank into Farley's belly. He followed it instantly with a right that smashed Farley's lips against his teeth.

Farley staggered back but Joseph didn't follow him. Handy said, "All right. The three of you get back into one of the cells."

Holloman, blood running down his arm from his shoulder wound and dripping from his fingers, glared murderously at Handy, then shuffled toward the barred door leading to the cells. Handy said, "Leave the knives on the desk."

Holloman drove his knife savagely into the desk. Farley, spitting teeth, staggered along behind him and followed suit. The other man laid his knife meekly beside the other two.

Joseph sat down and let his head hang between his knees. Handy herded the three men into a cell, then slammed and locked the door. Luke Kitchen stared at them with frightened eyes. Handy glanced at the body of the dead Indian before he returned to the office where Joseph was. Joseph looked up. "That was stupid of me."

"Anybody can make a mistake."

Joseph grinned at him. "You came up pretty tough."

"We're both going to have to be tough for the next few days."

"What are we going to do with the Indian?"

Handy frowned. He hadn't thought of that. He said, "Bury him, I suppose."

"The judge isn't due for a couple of weeks. There's time for me to take him back."

"Take him back? Are you crazy?"

"I could take him to Ma's village. Somebody there could probably tell me where he belongs."

19

Handy studied his son, probing the young man's expression, trying to gauge what was in his thoughts. He could see that returning the Indian to his own village for tribal burial was important to Joseph. He also knew it was dangerous but he nodded reluctantly anyway. "All right. Go get a couple of horses at the livery barn. Make a travois for him. I'll get the blacksmith to take off the irons."

Joseph went out into the street. The sun was dropping toward the horizon in the west. It cast long shadows from the Brown Hotel across the street, shadows that reached almost to the jail. Joseph headed down the street toward the tall, yellow frame livery barn across from Radinski's Hide Yard.

From the cell that held the three buffalo hunters, Holloman's voice came angrily, "You going to let me sit here and bleed to death?"

"No. I'll get the doc for you." Handy went out, pulling the door closed behind him and locking it. His horse was still tied in front. He mounted and rode up the street to Doc Bennett's house.

Doc's wife answered the door. She was a heavy-set woman past fifty, whose eyes betrayed her anger at the way he had forced the doctor to treat the Indian. Handy removed his hat. "There's a wounded man down at the jail, Mrs. Bennett, that I'd like Doc to come down and treat."

"Another red Indian?"

"No ma'am. A buffalo hunter. One of those that shot the Indian."

"What's the matter with him?"

He stared at her patiently. "Gunshot. He's bleeding. Will you tell the doc?"

For a moment he thought she would refuse. Then she

said grudgingly, "I'll tell him," and slammed the door. Handy walked out to his horse, untied him and mounted. He rode at a trot to the blacksmith shop right next to Sol Radinski's Hide Yard and across the street from the jail.

A plank ramp led up from the street. Handy did not dismount, but forced his horse up the hollow-sounding ramp.

Karl Spitzer, the blacksmith, was shoeing a horse. He had one of the horse's forefeet between his knees, fitting a shoe to it. He glanced up. Handy said, "Get whatever you're going to need and come over to the jail. I want those manacles off that Indian."

Spitzer released the horse's hoof. He straightened. There was a smoldering fire in the forge and the smoke from it burned Handy's eyes. Spitzer asked, "Is he dead?"

Handy nodded.

"Then what the hell do you want the manacles off for?"

"Joseph is going to take him back where he belongs."

"Are you crazy? You trying to start an Indian war?"

Spitzer raised a hand and wiped the sweat out of his eyes. He was naked to the waist and hairy-chested. Sweat gleamed where there was no hair. Handy said, "I'm not going to argue with you. Get your tools and come over to the jail."

"And if I won't?"

Handy's patience was wearing thin. "You'll take those manacles off or I'll throw you in the cell with the three buffalo hunters that brought him in."

"On what charge, for Christ's sake?"

"How about accessory to murder?"

"You couldn't make a thing like that stick in court

and you know it. All I did was put those irons on him."

"I don't have to make it stick. I can keep you in jail until the circuit judge gets here. That'll be two weeks at least."

Spitzer considered that. Shrugging, he said, "I've got to finish with this horse."

Handy shook his head. "Finish the horse afterward."

"God damn it . . . !"

"Finish the horse afterward."

Grumbling, Spitzer put the shoe back into the forge and slammed his tongs down on the floor. He got a hammer, a chisel and hacksaw and handed them up to the sheriff. He picked up a heavy portable anvil and staggered out with it.

Handy followed him across the street. Spitzer carried the anvil back to the cell where the dead Indian was and dropped it angrily on the floor. The sheriff dismounted and carried Spitzer's tools inside. He carried them as far as the cell door then threw them in on the floor beside the anvil. Spitzer turned his head to glare at him but after briefly meeting the sheriff's eyes, he let his own glance drop. Still grumbling, he picked up the tools and laid them on the bunk beside the dead Indian. He moved the anvil over close to the bunk and went to work.

Doc Bennett came in and Handy said, "It's that big buffalo hunter back there. Name of Holleman. He's shot through the shoulder. I'll let you in."

He followed Doc back to the cell that held the three and let him in. He locked the cell again. "That other one, Farley, has got some broken teeth but I don't suppose there's much you can do for him."

"I can pull the stubs."

Handy went out into the street. The sun had dropped behind the Brown Hotel and the front of the jail was in

22

its shade. The street was busier now than it had been all afternoon. Fifteen or twenty people were visible.

Joseph came up the street from the livery barn, leading his own saddled horse and another, to whose saddle a travois had been rigged out of two old wagon tongues. He tied both horses to the rail in front of the jail. Up the street several men turned to stare. Handy thought bitterly that even the decent people of the town had condoned the barbarous display in the window of the hardware store. Not a one of them had apparently objected to it.

Several of them gathered into a group to talk and almost immediately came hurrying down the street. Jared Brown, who owned the hotel, was their spokesman. He asked, "What are you doing, Pete?"

"Joseph is going to take the Indian back to his tribe. He died a little while ago."

Brown stared at him unbelievingly. "Are you out of your mind? Don't you know how that will affect the Indians?"

"Somebody should have thought of that before they let him be chained and displayed in the hardware store without even getting his wounds dressed first."

"We didn't put him there."

"And you didn't do anything to stop the three who did."

"What could we do? You're the sheriff and you were out of town."

Handy said, "There are at least fifty men in town. Fifty ought to have been able to stop three if they had really wanted to."

"Those buffalo hunters . . . no telling what they might have done if we had interfered."

Handy stared at him disgustedly. A flush crept into

23

Jared Brown's already florid face. He said angrily, "He was only an Indian."

"That's what my wife is, Brown. Only an Indian. And Joseph is half Indian."

"Don't blame us because your taste runs to . . ." Brown stopped suddenly. Handy's stare stayed riveted on his face. The flush in Brown's face deepened. He mumbled, "I'm sorry Pete. But damn it, you can't blame people for hating Indians. It's only been the last year or two that they've stopped butchering settlers."

Handy said, "I don't blame them. But what did the Indians ever do to you?"

"That's not the point. The point is that if you take this dead Indian back to them you're liable to start another Indian war."

"I guess that's a chance we'll have to take. He's entitled to be buried by his tribe."

"In the crotch of a goddam tree, I suppose."

"Something like that. Go see if Spitzer is about finished, Joseph."

Joseph went into the jail. The group of townsmen groped for something to say, something that would change the sheriff's mind. At last Brown said, "The people of this county elected you. You're supposed to do what they want you to."

Handy looked at him irritably. It had been a long day and he was tired. He was tired and he was angry. He said, "I'm not supposed to do what anyone wants me to. I'm supposed to uphold the law and keep the peace."

"You call taking that Indian back to his tribe keeping the peace?"

Before Handy could answer, Joseph came out of the jail. "He's on the last leg iron."

Handy said, "Go up to the restaurant and get yourself
24

something to eat."

Joseph headed up the street toward McDevitt's Restaurant. Handy turned and went into the jail. He slammed the door deliberately in the faces of the angry townsmen standing on the walk.

CHAPTER 4

McDevitt's Restaurant was on the corner of Chestnut and Main, diagonally across from the Indian Wells Hardware Store. Across Chestnut on the other corner was the Kansas Mercantile.

The eating place was owned by John McDevitt. Mrs. McDevitt did the cooking and their daughter, Oralee, waited on tables. McDevitt, himself, spent most of his time in the Free State Saloon.

Except for transient buffalo hunters and cowhands, the restaurant would have failed for lack of business. As it was, it made a living of sorts for the McDevitt family and it bought John McDevitt his whisky at the saloon.

Joseph sat down at a table in the corner. The smell of roasting beef was in the room and so was a light haze of cooking smoke and steam. Two buffalo hunters were eating noisily at another table. They looked at Joseph, scowled, then returned their attention to their food.

Oralee McDevitt came hurrying to Joseph's table. She was dressed today in a threadbare blue and white checked gingham dress that made her eyes look even bluer than usual. Her skin was white, freckled lightly across the bridge of her nose. Her hair was the color of dry prairie grass.

Joseph sometimes walked Oralee home. Sometimes he sat with her for a while on the porch steps of the

25

McDevitt house if her mother and father weren't at home. He had kissed her a few times and he was beginning to wonder if maybe he didn't want to marry her. Not that he seriously thought it possible. To the McDevitts he was Indian despite the fact that his father was white.

He said, "Hello Oralee."

"Hello Joseph. What are you going to have?"

Joseph reached out and caught her hand. "Hey! I've been gone three days and you don't even ask me if we caught up with Luke."

"I saw you and your father ride by with him."

"Then I guess you saw us with the Indian too."

She nodded, looking at the floor, a slight flush climbing into her face.

Joseph said, "He's dead. He died down at the jail."

"That's too bad." Her tone was nearly expressionless. A frown appeared on Joseph's face. He studied her closely as he said, "Too bad? Is that all?"

She lifted her glance. There was a quick impatience in her now. "What do you expect me to say? He was only a wild Indian."

Joseph said shortly, "That smells like roast beef. I guess you can bring me some." He dropped her hand.

She stood looking down at him for several moments. She seemed to want to say something but she didn't know what to say. At last she turned and hurried to the kitchen.

His mind reflected on her words, "wild Indian." He thought wryly that he must be what she'd call a "tame Indian," or maybe a "tame half Indian." He caught the buffalo hunters scowling at him again and scowled steadily back, forcing them to look away.

He supposed he wasn't being quite fair to Oralee. She

26

wasn't as prejudiced against Indians as she sounded or she wouldn't let him walk her home. She wouldn't have returned his kisses the way she had.

But he couldn't keep anger from smoldering in him. Oralee came back, bringing a glass of water and some silverware. She put them on the table, then abruptly sat down across from him. "I'm sorry, Joseph."

He felt an odd stubbornness. "For what?"

"For calling him a wild Indian. I know you're half Indian but I never think of you that way."

"How do you think of me?"

A flush crept up and stained her face.

He grinned, his irritation gone. He said, "That's how I think of you."

"Joseph!"

He kept his eyes fixed on her, the grin fading slowly. "I'm leaving town right after supper. Otherwise I'd walk you home."

"Where are you going now?"

"I'm taking the Indian back to his village for burial."

"Why don't you just bury him right here?"

"I figure he's entitled to an Indian burial. Without it, he's supposed to wander forever between the earth and sky.

"You know that isn't so."

"Isn't it? It's part of their religion."

"But they're only heathen savages."

"We never get away from that, do we? My mother is one of those heathen savages."

"Oh Joseph, I didn't mean . . ." She sighed impatiently. "Why can't we ever talk without arguing?"

From the kitchen Mrs. McDevitt shrilly called. "Oralee!" Oralee got to her feet. "Your supper's ready."

She went into the kitchen. She was gone several

27

minutes. When she returned she had a plate of steaming roast beef, potatoes, carrots, and a smaller plate of home-baked bread. She put them down.

One of the buffalo hunters said hoarsely, "Hey you!"

She crossed to their table, picked up their bread plate and went to the kitchen to refill it. Joseph began to eat. His throat hurt every time he swallowed from the abuse Farley had given it earlier in the jail.

The door opened and Jared Brown came in. He looked at Joseph, frowned, then nodded curtly and looked away again. He sat down with his back to Joseph at a table on the far side of the room.

Joseph ate doggedly, chewing, swallowing, drinking water to ease his bruised and tender throat. A third buffalo hunter came in and joined the other two.

The three kept glancing toward him. He knew they were resentful because he and his father had arrested Holloman, Farley, and Weigand but there was more to it than that. He wondered if the time would ever come when he would be accepted by the whites. He doubted it. He would probably spend his life as a kind of second-class citizen, tolerated but never trusted, permitted to live among them but never liked.

He was a fool if be thought he could ever get the job his father held. A man had to be elected to the sheriff's job. And who would vote for an Indian, or a half Indian, no matter how good he was or how much experience he had?

He finished the last bite of meat and mopped his plate with a piece of bread. Oralee brought him a cup of coffee, put it down, then hurried away to wait on Jared Brown and on the buffalo hunter who had come in after him.

A couple of cowhands came in. They glanced at

Joseph, nodded and sat down as far away from him as they could. Joseph thought irritably that they preferred the buffalo hunters' stink to sitting close to an Indian. Then he grinned wryly to himself. He was probably making all that up. He was so sure people were going to dislike and distrust him that he found dislike and distrust even when it wasn't there. He had a chip on his shoulder and went around just daring someone to knock it off.

He finished his coffee and put a quarter on the table. He waited several moments for Oralee. When she didn't appear, he got up and went outside, thinking that she had stayed in the kitchen deliberately because she didn't want to talk to him any more.

For several moments he stood on the boardwalk outside the restaurant, idly picking his teeth. The sun was below the horizon, but its afterglow had stained some high, puffy clouds in the west a brilliant orange. The air was beginning to chill. The leaves on the town's cottonwoods were a bright yellow that caught and held the afterglow from the flaming clouds.

Hatred of Indians had its roots in fear, he thought, and among the Indians, hatred of the whites also had its roots in fear. And it would be a long, long time before fear departed from frontier towns like Indian Wells or from the villages of the Indians.

Maybe it would be better for everybody if he just went back to the Indians. His father couldn't continue, indefinitely, to force him down the throats of the reluctant residents of Cheyenne County and of the town of Indian Wells. Sooner or later they'd balk. They'd either force Handy to resign or defeat him at the polls.

Looking down the street Joseph could see horses tied in front of the jail, one with a travois secured to the

29

saddle. He could see a small group of men in front of the Free State Saloon. He walked that way, wishing he could avoid this feeling of defiance whenever he approached a group of townspeople. At least, if he went back to live with the Indians, he'd feel like he belonged.

As he approached, the group went into the saloon. It was all too obvious that they did so to avoid speaking to him.

Joseph reached the jail and opened the door. Pete Handy sat in his ancient swivel chair, his booted feet up on the roll-top desk. The top of the desk was heavily scarred by his spurs.

Joseph said, "I guess I'm ready. Want to help me load him on the travois?"

The chair squeaked as Handy got to his feet. He studied his son's face, seeing the anger there. He didn't comment nor did he ask about the cause of it, but he supposed it had to do with Oralee. He knew Joseph was interested in her. He also knew it would never work. Neither Oralee's mother nor his father would accept Joseph as a son-in-law.

He walked back into the cell where the dead Indian was. Maybe he'd been wrong in trying to force Joseph to live in a white man's world. Joseph wasn't happy and he didn't fit. He never would, no matter how he tried.

Frowning, Handy lifted the dead Indian's upper half while Joseph took his legs. Holloman said sourly, from his cell, "I'm glad you're gettin' that damn dead meat out of here."

Handy turned his head. "If he was here a month he wouldn't smell any worse than you."

Joseph didn't speak and he didn't look up but Handy could see the cords straining in his neck. He could see the dull flush that had crept up into his face.

30

Joseph backed through the office and out the door into the street. The horses at the rail fidgeted and snorted and tried to pull away. Handy spoke soothingly to them. He and Joseph carried the dead Indian to the travois and laid him in it. Joseph got the lariat from his saddle and began to lash the body in place. Finished, he removed the bloody bandages from the Indian's wounds. The sunlight faded from the clouds. The sky turned gray. The street was deserted now. Joseph wondered where all the people had gone so suddenly.

Pete Handy looked at his son. "Give my best to your mother. Tell her I'm coming to see her as soon as I can."

"I'll tell her."

For an instant there was an unspoken closeness between the two. Handy said at last, almost reluctantly, "You be careful."

"Yeah."

Joseph untied both horses and swung to his saddle. Leading the horse to which the travois was lashed, he rode up the street toward the northern edge of town. In front of the Kansas Mercantile, he turned his head and raised a hand.

Handy locked the door of the jail. Then he headed up the street toward McDevitt's Restaurant to get his supper and to order meals for the prisoners.

CHAPTER 5

THE HORSE JOSEPH WAS LEADING WAS SKITTISH ABOUT the travois dragging along behind but by the time they reached the edge of town, he had accepted it and settled down. Dust raised both from the horses' hoofs and from the travois poles. Residents lined the upper end of Main. Joseph saw curtains being pulled aside so the occupants could look at him.

At the upper end of town, Main Street became a narrow, dusty road along which the twice weekly stagecoach departed for the East. A faint smell of dust hung over the road and Joseph knew that a horse or perhaps several had traveled it a short time ago.

His senses sharpened and his muscles tensed. The light was rapidly fading but there was still enough to see objects clearly at about a hundred yards.

He was not surprised when half a dozen mounted men rode out from behind a clump of willows and cottonwoods and halted in the road. He did not slow his pace nor did he touch his gun. When he was a dozen yards away he drew his horse reluctantly to a halt.

The men were Silas Grosbeck, Jared Brown, Karl Spitzer, John McDevitt, Sol Radinski, and Doc Bennett. Grosbeck was apparently their spokesman because he said, "Evenin', Joseph."

Joseph looked at him. "Evenin', Mr. Grosbeck." Grosbeck groped for words. At last he said, "You're doing a foolish thing."

"Taking this dead Indian back to his people for burial? It's an old custom, Mr. Grosbeck, that even whites observe."

Grosbeck's pale face flushed. He said, "I guess we deserved that, Joseph. And I guess we're ashamed of what we did to that Indian."

"You *guess?*"

Grosbeck's voice was sharper when he replied. "There's no use in going into it now, but I might remind you that it isn't only Indians that have suffered out here. There's hardly a family in Indian Wells that hasn't suffered something at the hands of the Indians."

Jared Brown, noticeably florid even in poor light, interjected irritably, "You're being bullheaded, Joseph. We'll give the Indian a decent burial. We'll even pay for it."

Joseph turned his head to look at Brown. "A decent *Christian* burial, Mr. Brown?"

Brown said defensively, "Getting unpleasant isn't going to get us anywhere."

"What will get us somewhere, Mr. Brown?" Joseph's anger, which had smoldered silently ever since he and his father had discovered the Indian in the window of the hardware store, now flared dangerously.

Brown started to reply but Grosbeck put out a hand and touched his arm. Brown's horse danced away and Grosbeck said, "Be reasonable, Joseph. That's all we ask."

Joseph stared at him. It was almost dark and he doubted if Grosbeck could see the expression on his face. He said, "You hypocrite. You showed this man, wounded, like a captured animal and because you did he's dead. Don't tell me to be reasonable."

"Joseph . . ."

"Get out of my way, Mr. Grosbeck. Unless you're ready to kill me too."

Sol Radinski broke in, his voice accented heavily, "Joseph, this you can't do to us. You know what the savages will do when they see this man, when they see what . . ."

"No, Mr. Radinski. What will they do?"

"They'll get up a war party to attack the town." Joseph said, "That's a chance." The light was now almost gone.

"About the town you don't care anything?"

Joseph looked at him bitterly. "Should I care? Have any of you ever let me forget that I am half Indian?"

"When your father made you his deputy, you swore to uphold the law."

Joseph didn't answer that. He was thinking that regardless of his lack of acceptance by the town, he still had a responsibility to the people of Indian Wells, to the people of the county, too. He *was* his father's deputy. But he wasn't breaking the law by taking the Indian home for burial. He said at last, "I'm not breaking any law, Mr. Radinski. I'm just trying to do what's right."

"Right? Is it right getting us killed? Is it right bringing savages down on us?"

Joseph shrugged. He did not intend to change his mind. He did not intend to return to town with the Indian. He said stubbornly, "Get out of the way."

"No! You're not going. Not while I can stop you." Radinski raised his gun.

Dark it was but there was still light enough for Joseph to be silhouetted against the sky, still light enough for him to see Radinski's rifle leveled and pointed straight at him. He touched his heels to his horse's sides. The very fact that the six men carried guns meant they had expected they might have to use force to make him stay. There was suddenly an empty feeling in his stomach. His heart felt as if some giant hand was squeezing it.

His horse moved ahead uncertainly. Joseph touched his sides again.

Radinski's voice was shrill and trembling. "Joseph!"

Joseph's horse reached those of the men obstructing him. Joseph guided his head between Radinski's horse and Grosbeck's. He was close enough to bat Radinski's rifle aside, but he made no attempt to do so. Head rigid, eyes straight ahead, he forced his horse between

34

Radinski's and Grosbeck's. They closed the gap slightly after he had passed but he dragged the other horse on through.

The temptation to spur his horse was great but he stubbornly resisted it. At a walk, he continued up the road. He did not look back.

All six of the men stared after him. Grosbeck whispered, "Shoot! God damn it, why don't you shoot?"

Radinski lowered the rifle. "How can I? His gun he wouldn't even draw."

"You yellow son-of-a-bitch!"

"Why don't you shoot him, Mr. Grosbeck? If you're so brave, why don't *you* shoot him?"

Grosbeck was silent, by his silence admitting what each of the six had known—that whoever shot Joseph would answer personally to Pete Handy for doing so. Joseph and his horses had disappeared. Brown said placatingly, "There's no point in calling names. Truth is, I guess none of us was ready for a showdown either with Joseph or his pa."

"Well, we'd better get ready for a showdown with the Indians. He'll bring the whole Cheyenne nation down on us."

"Maybe not. They'd have to be pretty stirred up to attack a town."

"And you think that boy's body won't stir them up? There's two bullet holes in it and there are burns on both ankles and both wrists from Spitzer's carelessness in putting on the irons."

Spitzer said, "Sure, sure, blame me. But if you'd been tryin' to put irons on him and he'd kept lookin' at you the way he was lookin' at me, you'd have hurried too."

Grosbeck said, "I don't know about the rest of you but I need a drink."

Jared Brown said, "Going to the saloon and getting full of whisky isn't going to help us any more than calling names. I think we ought to see Pete Handy. I think we ought to start thinking about getting some troopers from Fort Hays to help fight off the Indians."

"That's a damn good idea." All the men seemed to agree. There was relief in their voices as if the problem had been solved.

Brown led off toward town. The lights twinkled in the distance as they came off the narrow dirt road onto Main. They rode down the street abreast and reined their horses in at the hitch rail in front of the jail.

Grosbeck asked, "Who's going to do the talking?" Radinski said, "Let Jared do it."

There was a murmur of agreement as the men dismounted and tied their horses to the rail. Jared Brown went to the door, only to find it locked. There was a single, dim lamp burning inside the jail.

Brown jumped guiltily as a voice from the darkness said, "Looking for something, gentlemen?" He swung around.

Pete Handy's shape loomed up in the darkness, coming almost silently down the walk. Brown said, "We want to talk to you."

"Sure. Come on in. Here, Jared. Hold these trays." The sheriff handed Brown four stacked up trays. They were heavy and they were hot. Handy unlocked the door, went in and turned up the lamp. He took the four trays from Brown. He put them on the desk. "You don't mind waiting while I feed the prisoners, do you?"

All six men grunted something to the effect that they did not. Handy took Kitchen's tray back first. He unlocked the cell and put it on the floor. He backed out and locked the cell again.

He lighted the lamp at the end of the corridor between the cells before he went back for the other trays. He brought them back and put them down on the floor outside the cell. The buffalo hunters started toward the door, but Handy said, "Huh uh. You three sit down. I'll bring the trays in and put them on the floor. You can come for them after the door is locked again."

Holloman asked unpleasantly, "Scared of us, Sheriff?"

Handy looked at him. He didn't speak for a moment. When he did, he just said, "No." The hunters sat down on the bunk and Handy unlocked the door. He put the three trays on the floor inside the cell, then backed out and locked it again.

He returned to the office where the six men waited for him. He stared at Brown. "Well?"

"That was a pretty stupid thing—letting Joseph take that Indian's body back."

"It was stupid of you to let the Indian die. I don't blame you for the fact that he was shot. That happened outside of town and you had nothing to do with it. But I do blame you for letting him lie in Grosbeck's window. How long was he in there, anyway?"

Brown said, "Only a day or two."

"*Only* a day or two?"

"Well . . . they brought him in the same day you left."

"Then it was three days."

The six men stared at him sullenly. At last Brown said, "We want you to send for troops. If a man left right away, he could get to Fort Hays before noon tomorrow. The troops could get here before the Indians do."

Handy said, "You don't know any Indians are coming here."

"Maybe not, but there's a damn good chance they are." Handy stared sourly at him. "It'd serve you right if they did come here."

"That's a hell of a thing to say!"

Handy did not reply. The silence ran on for what seemed like a long, long time. At last Radinski asked, "Well? What about it? Are you going to send for troops?"

Handy sat down in his swivel chair. He took out his pipe and packed it deliberately as if he was all alone. He lighted it and filled the room with clouds of bluish smoke. He said, "No."

"No?" Radinski's voice was excited and outraged. "What do you mean, no? This town's in danger and it's up to you to see that something's done."

Handy looked at him steadily through the haze of smoke.

Radinski glanced helplessly at Jared Brown. He and Grosbeck were scowling angrily. So was Karl Spitzer, the blacksmith. Doc Bennett and John McDevitt looked helpless and confused.

Brown said, "It's plain enough that we're not making any progress here. Let's go, gentlemen. We're going to have to take care of this ourselves."

He turned, fat and florid, and waddled to the door. The others followed him. Spitzer, the last man out, started to slam the door. He caught Handy looking at him and closed it quietly.

The six mounted their horses and rode up the street toward the Free State Saloon. Frowning, Handy puffed on his pipe, worrying about Joseph's safety and wondering how all this was going to end.

CHAPTEIR 6

THE SIX TOWNSPEOPLE DISMOUNTED IN FRONT OF THE Free State Saloon. They tied their horses to the rail. Carrying rifles and shotguns, they trooped inside.

Lamps in the overhead chandelier were burning. So were the lamps on the backbar. Four buffalo hunters sat at a table in one corner, playing cards. A couple of cowhands were talking down at the end of the bar. Tony Gallo was behind the bar. He wore a limp, sweat-stained blue shirt and a dirty white apron. Jared Brown looked at him with unconcealed distaste.

Gallo took a swipe at the bar with a dirty rag. "What'll it be, gents?"

Brown said, "Whisky. And none of that rotgut you sell the buffalo hunters."

Gallo brought a bottle from beneath the bar. He put it in front of Brown. "That suit you, Mr. Brown?"

Brown scowled at his tone. Gallo set out six glasses. Brown poured his own glass full, then passed the bottle to John McDevitt, next to him. Gallo waited and finally Brown said irritably, "We'll call you if we need anything else."

Gallo said, "Yes *sir*, Mr. Brown." He moved away down the bar and stopped to talk to the two cowhands.

Brown said, "Who are we going to send?"

Nobody answered him. Doc Bennett sat staring at the glass in front of him. There was a slight frown on his face. Brown said, "It ought to be someone that rides a lot." He turned his head and stared at Spitzer, "How about your boy?"

"Can't spare him."

39

"Well, you'd better spare him. Unless you can think of somebody else."

Spitzer nodded grudgingly.

"Go get him then. I'll write the letter," Brown said. Spitzer gulped his drink, turned and went out into the street. He untied his horse and mounted. He rode along Maple to Second Avenue, then turned right toward Indian Creek. His house, one of the few in town that was built of logs, faced Elm and had its back to the alley behind the jail.

He lived with his wife, Sarah, and his son, Tom, who was fourteen. Spitzer tied his horse to the hitching post in front and went up the walk. A breeze, blowing from the hide yard, made him wrinkle his nose with distaste. His blacksmith shop was next to the hide yard and he smelled that stink all day. It seemed like when he went home at night he ought to be able to get away from it.

He felt irritable. Wondering why, he decided that it was probably the way Jared Brown always took charge of things, issuing orders like he was some kind of goddam Army officer or something. He went around to the back door. He pumped a basin of water and washed before he went into the house.

His wife, standing at the stove, turned to look at him. "You're late."

"Yeah." He did not offer to explain.

"It will be on in a minute. Are you washed?"

"Yeah. Where's Tom?"

"He's out in the stable."

Spitzer went to the door. He stuck his head out and shouted, "Tom!" He returned to the table and sat down. After a moment, Tom came in. He looked at his father, his face expressionless but somehow disapproving too. Spitzer asked, "What the hell's the matter with you?"

40

"Nothing."

"Then don't look at me like that." He knew what was bothering Tom. The boy had come into the blacksmith shop when he was putting irons on the Indian. He thought about it a moment, growing more irritated all the time. He finally said angrily, "I got to take what jobs come in. We ain't so goddam much that I can turn customers away."

Tom did not reply. Spitzer stared at him challengingly for several moments but Tom did not look up.

Sarah set the table and began to put the food on. When she had finished she sat down. Spitzer, scowling, bowed his bead. "We thank thee Lord for this food." He tucked his napkin into his collar and began to eat. His hands were hard and broad and callused. There was black dirt under his fingernails.

After a while he said, "We had a meeting at the saloon. We want you to ride to Fort Hays and deliver a letter." Tom looked up, interest in his face. "What for? What's the letter say?"

"It's a request for troops. Handy's half-breed son took that dead Indian back to his village for burial. We think there's a chance the Indians may try to get revenge."

"Sure, Pa. Sure, I'll go." Tom was silent a moment and then he said, "Gee," his voice touched with awe.

Sarah's worried eyes clung to Spitzer's face. He continued to eat, feeling her regard. Finally he glanced up at her. "It ain't nothing to get yourself all riled up about. We don't know the Indians are coming here. We just figure we ought to be ready if they do."

"Will Tom . . . ?"

"He'll be all right. There ain't no Indians between here an' Hays."

Tom asked, "Can I ride my own horse?"

41

"All right. Finish your supper and saddle him. Sarah, fix him a sack of food."

Tom gulped what remained of his supper, got his coat and hurried out. Sarah began to put some food into a sack. Spitzer finished his supper. He got up, frowning again, wondering why he couldn't forget what it had been like taking the manacles off the dead Indian. He took the sack of food and went out the back door. Tom was waiting beside his horse. Spitzer handed him the sack of food. He said, "It ain't hard to find Fort Hays. You head south. The first river you come to is the North Fork of the Solomon. Next is the South Fork and after that the Saline. After that you come to Big Creek and you follow that east until you reach Fort Hays."

"I ain't goin' to have no trouble, Pa." But Tom's voice vibrated with excitement and nervousness.

"All right then. Get up on your horse and come down to the saloon. Jared Brown said he'd have the letter ready when we got there."

He walked around to the front of the house. Tom followed him. Spitzer untied his own horse and mounted. He led out toward the saloon. He suddenly had a compulsion to try and explain to Tom about the manacles. But what could he say? The buffalo hunters had wanted manacles on the Indian and had paid him to put them there. There wasn't anything beyond that to explain.

He reached the Free State Saloon, got down and tied his horse. He went in, with Tom following timidly. Inside, Tom looked around with youthful interest.

Brown called him to the bar and handed him the letter. He said, "I'll give you two dollars for making the trip when you get back."

Tom nodded, too excited to speak. He looked at his

father and Spitzer nodded. Tom went out and Spitzer followed him.

Tom untied his horse and mounted. Spitzer said, "Tom."

"What?"

"I . . . Never mind." He handed his rifle up. "Be careful."

Spitzer stared moodily after him. Down on the other side of the jail he could see the dim lights of the town's two brothels. He caught the silhouetted shape of a woman in one of the windows, looking out. He shrugged, turned, and went back into the saloon.

John McDevitt was scowling at the drink in front of him. Spitzer knew that Joseph Handy had been seeing Oralee McDevitt, walking her home, sitting on the porch steps with her, and he supposed that was what was bothering McDevitt now. Sol Radinski said, as if repeating something he had been saying over and over in his mind. "We should have stopped Joseph. We shouldn't have let him go."

Grosbeck said, "You had your chance. You had a gun on him."

Spitzer poured his glass full and gulped the whisky down. He poured another and stood looking sourly at it. He glanced at Grosbeck, suddenly wondering what he had ever seen in Grosbeck to like. Grosbeck felt his glance, turned his head and met it with level eyes. "What the hell's the matter with you? You put the irons on him."

Brown said, "Stop it! Bickering among ourselves isn't going to get us anyplace. We all ought to be ashamed. We let that wounded Indian lie in Grosbeck's store window for three whole days. Not one of us tried to put a stop to it. What we'd better hope is that the story don't leak out. You can imagine what the Eastern newspapers would do with a thing like that. It'd ruin Indian Wells. It'd ruin all of us."

Doc Bennett said, "Tom should have been warned. Nobody told him not to say anything."

Spitzer said, "He won't say anything."

"How the hell do you know?"

"He's my boy. That's how I know."

Bennett snorted, unconvinced.

Brown said, "There's another thing. When the troops get here the story will sure as hell leak out. Unless everyone in town is told to keep their damn mouths shut."

Grosbeck stared unbelievingly at the group. "You're all crazy if you think you can keep what happened from leaking out. Have you forgotten that Pete Handy has those three buffalo hunters down there in jail, holding them for trial? When the circuit judge gets here the whole story's got to come out. It doesn't matter if Tom Spitzer talks down at Fort Hays. It doesn't matter what anybody tells the soldiers when they arrive. Because that story's going to come out as soon as the buffalo hunters' trial begins."

Brown said, "Maybe we can talk Handy out of holding them. Maybe he'd be willing to just run them out of town if he knew how serious it would be for the town to have this story get into the papers back East."

Grosbeck said contemptuously, "Nobody's likely to talk Pete Handy out of anything."

Frowning, Brown said, "Doc, why don't you and me go down and try? He might be reasonable."

Doc shrugged. "All right. I ought to look at that buffalo hunter anyway."

Brown glanced at the other four. He started to say

44

something, then changed his mind. McDevitt finished his drink, wiped his mouth with the back of his hand and followed Brown and Doc out into the street. He left them, turning toward his restaurant.

Brown and Doc Bennett walked down the street to the jail. There was a single lamp burning in the sheriff's office. Handy sat with his booted feet on the desk, a stubby pipe clenched between his teeth.

Doc Bennett glanced in through the open door at him. Nobody was going to make Handy release his prisoners, he thought. He and Brown were wasting their time and breath. Handy sat there like a rock, staring through a haze of bluish smoke. His hair was like an aging lion's mane. His face seemed dark as mahogany, framed as it was by graying hair.

As they came in, Handy put his feet down on the floor. He took the pipe out of his mouth. The chair squeaked noisily.

Handy wasn't nearly as tall as he seemed, Doc Bennett thought. Most men, after meeting him once, would have said he was over six feet tall. Truth was, he was only five feet nine. But he was thick through the chest and broad of shoulder and he had a commanding presence that made him seem even bigger than he really was.

Handy said, "I take it you sent for troops. I saw Tom Spitzer ride by a little while ago."

Brown nodded. He didn't know why he always felt on the defensive with Handy. He said, "Pete, we want to ask a favor of you."

"Sure. What is it?"

"We want you to release those three buffalo hunters and just run them out of town."

Handy started to refuse but Brown said hastily, "Now

45

wait a minute, Pete. Wait until you hear what we have to say.

Handy waited. Brown looked at Doc Bennett as though for reassurance before he said, "We've been talking it over. We've decided it can just about ruin this town and everyone in it if the story of that Indian gets printed in the newspapers in Kansas City and St. Louis. It'll make us all look mighty bad. The town won't live it down for a dozen years."

Handy put his pipe into his mouth and puffed on it without success. He struck a match on the side of the desk and relighted it. He puffed a moment before he glanced up. "You should have thought of that three days ago."

"Pete, he was only an Indian. Is his death that important? He'd likely have died anyway, whether or not he was put into that store window in irons."

"That's something we'll never know."

"Pete, for God's sake! The town's starting to grow. Last year four new families moved out here. But let that Indian thing get out and everybody's going to think we're a bunch of savages."

Handy got slowly to his feet. He said, "Jared, you know I can't let those buffalo hunters go. Not without a trial. They shot a man. A man, even if he was an Indian. They shot him for no reason, just for the goddam fun of it. And then, as if that wasn't bad enough, they put him in Grosbeck's store window like he was a coyote or a wolf. No sir, those buffalo hunters have got to go to trial."

Brown turned his head and looked helplessly at Doc. Doc asked wearily, "How's the big one, Pete?"

Handy said, "Mean as a bear in a trap. Let him alone, Doc. He'll be all right until tomorrow."

Brown and Doc Bennett shifted their feet and tried to meet the sheriff's eyes. Then, mumbling their grudging goodbyes, they turned and went out into the street. Brown pulled the door closed, wanting to slam it but afraid.

CHAPTER 7

FOR SEVERAL MINUTES AFTER LEAVING THE SIX townsmen behind, Joseph felt shaky and weak. He had expected a bullet to strike him in the back. Now he realized how tense he had become, as if taut muscles could turn a bullet aside. He grinned nervously to himself.

It had all been a bluff. They had hoped they could make him turn back by threatening him but none of them had been ready to go through with it. They were too afraid of Pete Handy for that. They had known that if they shot Handy's son they would have to face Handy afterward.

The travois made a monotonous, scratching sound. Joseph let the horses plod along at a steady walk. Frowning, he considered all the things that had happened this afternoon.

He had the feeling that powerful forces had been set in motion today, forces that could not be stopped. A chill touched his spine and spread, until his whole body suddenly felt cold. He scoffed inwardly at himself, calling his uneasiness primitive superstition, something inherited from the Indians. But it wouldn't go away. Even after the chill had passed, the uneasiness remained.

He halted and for a moment hesitated between

47

returning to Indian Wells and going on. He decided that he would not go back. He would not let the men of Indian Wells know that they had won. He kicked his horse into that plodding walk again. He began to think of the Indian villages.

A faint smile touched his mouth. It stayed briefly, then went away. In many ways he wanted to return to the Indian villages. But what would his father do if he went back to them?

He rode through the night, sometimes frowning at his thoughts, sometimes smiling at a pleasant memory. Dawn found him thirty-five miles north of Indian Wells, still fifteen or twenty miles short of the village where his mother lived. He urged his horse to a trot and kept him at that gait until he began to sweat. Then he let him walk again.

He saw but three buffalo between dawn and the time he rode into the village of Half Yellow Face. Three buffalo, he thought resentfully. And the plains had once been black with them. No wonder the Indians hated all white men. White men killed the buffalo only for their hides, leaving the meat to rot. And when the Indians needed meat, none was to be found anywhere.

Children ran out to meet him as he neared the village where his mother lived. Even in his white man's clothes, they recognized him. They let him go ahead and followed in the dusty wake of the travois, staring at the lashed-in body of the dead Indian.

At the edge of the village, adults joined the children following the travois. They talked quietly among themselves, pointing at the marks on the dead brave's wrists, pointing at the ugly wounds in his chest and thigh.

None called a greeting to Joseph, though all these

people knew him well. Nor did he greet them.

At his mother's tipi, he swung stiffly to the ground, tired from his sleepless night. He dropped his horse's reins and the animal stood fast, in spite of his obvious uneasiness over the smells of this strange and foreign place.

Joseph pushed aside the entrance flap and stepped inside. His mother, kneeling before the fire in the center of the lodge, glanced up at him.

For an instant she remained there, frozen by surprise. Then her face lighted with her smile. "Joseph!"

She got to her feet. She was a tall woman and strongly built. Her hair was black and untouched with gray. It hung in long braids, one over each of her firm, full breasts. Her face, dark from being much in the sun, was smooth and virtually unlined. Joseph crossed the tipi to her and put his arms around her. She hugged him briefly, then released him and looked up at him. "Did your father . . . ?"

"He didn't come. He said to tell you he would see you as soon as he could."

The excitement that had been in her eyes faded suddenly. He felt a catch in his throat. He wondered if he would ever be loved the way his father was. Answering the question in her eyes he said, "A young Indian was killed by some buffalo hunters near Indian Wells. He died yesterday and I'm taking him home for burial."

"A young man from here?"

He shook his head. "I thought someone here might recognize him and be able to tell me where he belongs."

"Let us go and see." She crossed the tipi to the flap, pushed it aside and stepped outside. Already a sizable crowd had gathered around the travois.

Bird Woman pushed through the crowd until she could see the dead Indian. She saw his wounds first, the one in his chest, the one in his thigh. She saw his pallor and knew he had lost much blood before he died.

Then she saw the marks of the manacles. Having lived with the whites, she knew instantly what they were. She also saw the burns that had resulted from Karl Spitzer's haste and carelessness.

Fear touched her as she glanced at Joseph's face. She asked, in English so that the villagers wouldn't understand, "Why did you bring him here? Why are you taking him home for burial? Don't you realize how dangerous it is?"

He glanced at her. He didn't answer but she could see that he fully understood all the possible consequences of his bringing the Indian's body home. She said, "You are being very foolish. Did not your father tell you this?"

Joseph grinned unexpectedly. "He wanted to, I guess."

"You are my son as well as your father's but your Indian blood will not be enough to save your life. Leave him here. Some of the men will take him where he belongs. Go back to Indian Wells."

Joseph said, "You know I can't. I've come this far and I've got to go through with it."

Bird Woman looked at him sadly. Joseph faced the crowd and spoke in the Cheyenne tongue. "This man was killed near a white man's village a day's ride to the south. I wish to take him to his own village so that he can be buried in the Cheyenne way. Does any one of you recognize him and know where his village is?"

An old man with a lined face and hair that was almost white, raised his head. "He is Fat Bear from the village of Spotted Horse. His father is Buffalo Hump."

50

Joseph looked at Bird Woman. She said, "The village of Spotted Horse is north and west on Red Willow Creek. It is half a day's ride from here."

He looked around at the faces of the villagers. Anger was apparent in them all. And suddenly Joseph felt like a stranger in spite of his Cheyenne blood, in spite of the fact that he had spent more years here than he had spent with the whites.

There was hostility and blame in the faces of the villagers, as if he had killed the young brave himself. There was smoldering anger in the eyes of the men. One of these, Badger, walked to the travois and picked up one of the dead man's hands. He looked at Joseph, scowling. "What is this?" he asked in the Cheyenne tongue, pointing to the marks of the manacles and to the burns and bruises made putting them on and removing them.

Joseph met Badger's stare steadily. It wasn't an easy thing for him to do. He said, "The white man tied his hands and feet with straps of iron and chains."

"Why? What had Fat Bear done?"

"I do not know. My father and I were trailing a murderer. When we got back, we found Fat Bear like this."

"He must have done something. Had he killed a white man?"

Joseph shook his head. "It was said that he was wounded in a fight with some buffalo hunters. He was captured."

"And even with the two wounds I see, he was tied with straps of iron and chains? They must have been much afraid of him. Where did they put him after they tied his hands and feet with iron? Did they put him in the white men's jail?"

Joseph shook his head. "They put him in the window of a store." He said it almost defiantly as if by bluntly telling the truth he could purge himself of his own feeling of guilt over the way the young Indian had died.

An old man in the crowd said, "I have been to the white men's villages. I have seen these windows he talks about. They are like a tipi wall but they are as clear as water and a man can see through them as if they weren't there."

Badger stared angrily at Joseph. "And the white men came to look at Fat Bear as he lay wounded behind this thing?"

Joseph nodded. "They came to look at him."

"And you did nothing?"

"I was not there. When I did arrive, with my father the sheriff, we took him from the window and called the medicine man to treat his wounds."

"Did you have the iron and chains removed?"

"Yes. After he had died."

"And what of the men who shot him and put the chains on him?"

"They are in the white men's jail. My father, the sheriff, is guarding them."

"What will be done with them?" Badger's voice was angry and insistent.

Joseph said, "They will be tried in the white men's court as soon as the judge arrives."

"And when will that be?"

"Two weeks from now." The Indian way of saying it was fourteen sleeps.

Badger paced up and down several times, his steps short and rapid. He stopped, turned his head and scowled at Joseph. "Will they be punished for killing Fat Bear?"

It would have been easy for Joseph to lie, for him to say they would. But he couldn't lie. That was his Indian training, he supposed. An Indian never lied. He said, "I do not know."

"Why do you not know?"

"It will depend on how the fight in which Fat Bear was shot took place."

"Will the white men's judge believe that Fat Bear, all alone, attacked the three white men?"

Joseph said, "I do not know."

"Do you believe Fat Bear attacked the three white men?"

Joseph shook his head.

"Why do you believe they shot Fat Bear?"

Joseph now scowled back. "I'm not going to guess about a thing like that."

"Why do you believe they shot Fat Bear? For no other reason than because he was an Indian and an enemy?"

Joseph nodded wearily. "Probably."

Badger said, "Go then. Take Fat Bear's body to his village."

His words were followed by a low, angry murmur from the crowd. Joseph mounted his horse, holding the reins of the other one. He tried to ignore the increasing hostility of the crowd. He looked at his moher. There was fear in her eyes, as if she did not believe she would ever see him again.

He reined his horse around and rode out of the village toward the north. The angry voices of the people followed him.

There was now an awful heaviness in his heart. The whites did not want him in Indian Wells. The Indians did not want him here.

CHAPTER 8

JOSEPH STRUCK RED WILLOW CREEK IN midafternoon, traveling alternately at a trot and at a walk. He wanted to reach the dead Indian's village as near dusk as possible. He might need darkness to effect his escape from the dead man's friends and relatives.

News of his coming would have preceded him. Not long after leaving his mother's village, he had seen a galloping brave briefly atop a distant ridge. Badger, he supposed.

Following the twisting course of Red Willow Creek, he came at last to the village of Spotted Horse.

It was a larger village than that in which his mother lived, comprising nearly a hundred tipis. They were formed in a semicircle on the bank of Red Willow Creek.

Joseph came down off a shallow rise which he had ascended to cut off a bend in the creek and saw the people assembled along its bank. He saw Badger standing beside his horse. He saw the ceremonial headdresses worn by the chiefs and medicine men.

They turned to face toward him while he was still a quarter mile away. Joseph felt a painful hollowness in his chest. His hand, holding the horse's reins, trembled slightly, and he rested it on the saddlehorn to steady it. He didn't want them to know he was nervous. He didn't want them to believe he was afraid.

He drew his horse to a halt a dozen yards from them. He recognized Spotted Horse, having seen him once when he was a boy. He looked straight at the chief and said, "I have brought home the body of Fat Bear for

54

burial."

The faces of the assembled Indians were angry and Joseph knew Badger had been talking to them. Some women began to wail softly in a minor key, a death chant for Fat Bear. The sound seemed to intensify the anger in the faces of the younger men.

Badger raised his voice to shout, "Tell them! Tell them how Fat Bear was wounded. Tell them about the irons and chains with which he was tied. Tell them how the white men displayed him, as if he was some kind of prairie animal."

Joseph said, "Fat Bear was shot in a fight with three buffalo hunters. He was brought to the town of Indian Wells and chains were put on his hands and feet. He was kept behind a window in one of the buildings there. When my father and I returned from pursuing a murderer, we found him and took him out. We called the medicine man for him but it was too late. He died that afternoon."

Badger shouted, "Tell them of the three who killed Fat Bear. Tell them they will be punished for their crime."

Joseph said evenly, "The three men who killed Fat Bear are in the white men's jail. My father is guarding them. They will be brought to trial in fourteen sleeps when the judge arrives."

Spotted Horse, nearly six feet tall, cleared his throat. He asked, "How will the white men punish them?" Joseph wished he could say the three would be hanged for their crime. Or that they would be confined for many years in the white men's prison. He wished he could lie but he could not. He said, "I do not know. That is for the judge and jury to decide at the trial."

Spotted Horse asked, "And what is this trial, of which

you speak?"

"It is like a council among the Indians. It is where the white men decide how they will punish someone who has broken one of their laws."

Spotted Horse said, "If an Indian killed a white man, we might decide not to punish him at all."

Joseph nodded. "The white men might decide not to punish the men who killed Fat Bear."

The wailing of the women was louder now. More women were wailing, out of sympathy for the bereaved. There was angry grumbling among the assembled Indians but so far no threats of violence. Women cut the ropes securing the body of Fat Bear in the travois. His father, Buffalo Hump lifted the body of his son and carried him away. The crowd began sullenly to disperse. Badger's face turned a darker red. He shouted, "How do we know that what this half-white man says is true? How do we know that he did not kill Fat Bear himself, and blame it on three buffalo hunters who do not exist?"

The crowd, their attention arrested, now turned back to face Joseph once again. He glanced at Badger and saw the maliciousness in Badger's eyes. One of the young men close to Joseph yelled, "Yes! How do we know he did not kill Fat Bear himself?"

The sun was sliding below the horizon in the west. Joseph tensed, now glad he had planned the time of his arrival as he had. But he didn't dare whirl and run. That would only precipitate a chase.

Neither did he want to stay because it now was plain that Badger was determined to incite the young braves to violence. He turned his horse and rode deliberately away, leading the horse to which the travois still was tied. He resisted a desire to look around.

Badger shouted, "Come back, murderer! Come back

56

and tell his relatives why you killed Fat Bear! Tell them why you came all this way to lie to them!"

Joseph heard a shout, and another, and another still. He heard the commotion, the murmur of the assembled crowd of Indians. He turned his head.

Half a dozen young men were running through the village toward the horse herd on the other side of Red Willow Creek. Badger had mounted and was riding with them, yelling at them to hurry or the killer would escape. Joseph released the reins of the horse he was leading. He touched spurs to his own mount's sides. There was no longer any need to maintain a deliberate pace.

His horse broke into a lope and as Joseph continued to rake him with the spurs, into a run. Joseph leaned low over his withers. At the crest of the rise he glanced behind again.

Two braves had caught horses and were racing across the creek, splashing water high. Three others were mounting. Badger, surprisingly, made no move to accompany them. He was riding back toward the village at a trot.

Then Joseph was below the crest of the rise, hidden from the village and from the men pursuing him. He raked his horse again, glancing toward the sun setting in the west.

Half an hour of daylight still remained. During that half hour he had to put as much distance as possible between himself and the pursuing Indians. Even if he exhausted his horse doing it.

Thinking of Badger, he frowned. Badger seemed to be more interested in staying in Spotted Horse's village than he was in catching him. To Joseph that meant just one thing. Badger would try to stir the older village warriors up just as he had stirred the young men up. Badger wanted the warfare between whites and Indians resumed.

Two galloping braves came over the rise and yelped shrilly when they saw Joseph ahead of them. Riding wildly and recklessly, they belabored their horses in an attempt to make them run faster still. They began to gain on Joseph, whose horse was tired from traveling all last night and all day today.

Joseph raked him even more savagely with the spurs. If he was going to lose the pursuit when darkness came it was essential that he stay at least a quarter mile ahead.

The other three young Indians came over the rise and yelped as the first two had done. These three came racing after the other two, trying to close the distance separating them.

They were no more than three quarters of a mile behind. All afterglow from the setting sun had faded from the clouds and the sky was wholly gray. The young braves were gaining steadily. They had spread out and had stopped yelling. They knew as well as Joseph did how near darkness was.

Joseph looked critically at his horse. The animal's neck was soaked with sweat. His breathing was labored. If he stumbled, or faltered . . .

Why had he really brought the dead Indian home for burial? Joseph asked himself. Had he been as concerned as he had claimed to be that the brave be buried according to Indian custom and belief?

He wryly admitted that he had not. That might have been part of it but he had also been punishing the inhabitants of Indian Wells for their barbarity in permitting the wounded Indian to be displayed. He had, in some deep recess of his mind, hoped the Indians would come to Indian Wells to avenge the death of the young Indian. And, consciously or unconsciously, he had wanted to get even with the town for the way they had treated him.

He glanced behind again. The leading two Indians were now a scant half mile behind. He admitted there was a chance that he was going to get caught. If he was, the price for his foolishness in bringing Fat Bear home was going to be exorbitant.

But if he was caught, wouldn't that satisfy the Indians? Wouldn't they refuse to be taunted into making an attack on Indian Wells?

He shook his head. It was more likely that his death would whet their appetite for blood. Spotted Horse and the other chiefs might try to keep the warriors in check, knowing another war with the whites could only result in a mass slaughter of the Indians, but it was doubtful if they could.

It was now too dark to clearly see objects more than a dozen yards away. Joseph let the horse have his head, trusting the animal's eyesight more than he did his own. He could no longer see the Indians pursuing him and they could not see him. They were trailing him now but soon the light would be too poor even for that.

His horse was faltering. Once he stumbled and nearly threw Joseph off. He recovered and went on, still faltering. As soon as it was too dark for the Indians to continue trailing him, Joseph slowed the animal to a walk. He also changed course, angling sharply to the right. It was possible that they had slowed or stopped as soon as it became too dark to trail, counting on following him by the sounds made by his galloping horse's hoofs. Or they might be coming on headlong, hoping to be lucky enough to overtake him in the dark.

He heard them go by, galloping, the two who had been closest to him. Waiting, his horse halted and silent, he heard the other three gallop by hard on the heels of the two. He waited several moments more, then continued at a walk, still angling away from his original course toward Indian Wells.

He had lost them in the dark but he knew he still was far from safe. He would circle and approach Indian Wells from the west. Even so there was a chance he would blunder into them.

He let the weary horse choose his own pace, let him cool off and let his breathing become slow and normal again. The hours slowly passed and even though his horse was tired, Joseph made better time returning than he had going because he had no travois to slow him down.

At dawn he rode across the marshy flat where the three springs that combined to form Indian Creek rose out of the ground and stared at the sleeping town.

He had no idea where the five young Indians were. There was a good chance they were within a quarter mile of him right now.

But they wouldn't attack the town. Not yet. They would wait and watch until reinforcements arrived from the village of Spotted Horse. Only when they thought there was a chance of defeating the whites would they attack the town.

Joseph heeled his horse down the slope toward the gray, untidily sprawling town. But it wasn't like coming home and he admitted suddenly that Indian Wells had never been home to him. He didn't think it ever would.

CHAPTER 9

AFTER JARED BROWN AND DOC BENNETT HAD LEFT the jail, Pete Handy went back to the cells and gathered up the dirty dishes and trays. He ignored Sime Holloman's baleful stare. Carrying the trays, he went through the office and out the door onto the walk. Putting them down, he carefully locked the door, then picked them up again and headed toward McDevitt's Restaurant.

The air had chilled the moment the sun went down and now it had a frosty smell. Fragrant smoke from cooking fires hung in a layer close to the ground. The smells and the chill reminded him that winter was on its way. Thinking of that, he remembered what winter had been like in the village of Half Yellow Face when Joseph was a little boy, when he and Bird Woman had been together all the time.

He shook his head impatiently, trying to drive away that nostalgic memory. He had made his choice. Besides, he knew that no one can ever go back in time. The past can never be regained.

He reached the restaurant and carried the trays inside. He put them down on a table, then sat at another. When Oralee came from the kitchen he said, "Bring me a cup of coffee, Oralee, if there's any left."

There had been talking in the kitchen when he came in but it stopped the minute she went back into the kitchen for his coffee. She brought it to him and started to return. Handy stopped her, saying, "Wait a minute, Oralee. I want to talk to you."

She looked at him with frightened wariness and he

61

grinned, "You look like I was going to bite. I'm not."
Oralee smiled nervously. Handy asked, "What do your
folks think about you going with Joseph, Oralee?"

Her face flushed painfully. Handy said, "They don't
like it, do they?"

Mutely she shook her head.

Handy asked, "Have they told you to stop seeing
him?"

She nodded, refusing to meet his glance.

"And you're going to?"

"I have to, Mr. Handy. I've got to do what Papa
says."

Handy nodded. He could see that there was no
strength in Oralee. She was pretty and sweet but there
was no strength in her. She asked timidly, "Can I go
now, Mr. Handy?"

He nodded, frowning faintly to himself. He finished
his coffee hurriedly, got up and went outside. There was
no strength in any of Oralee's family, he thought,
though her mother was probably the strongest of the
three. Still, a young man doesn't choose a girl for
strength. There are other things he thinks about.

He walked slowly down the street toward the jail.
Lamps were burning inside the Free State Saloon and
the place was crowded with noisy men. He glanced in
but he didn't stop. He didn't want to talk to anybody
now. He felt gloomy and depressed as if he had some
foreknowledge of disaster or of death. He shook himself
impatiently as if by so doing he could shake the feeling
off.

He went into the jail. Holloman began yelling for him
immediately. He went back to Holloman's cell. "What
do you want?"

"God damn it, this shoulder is killing me. Can't you

62

get that sawbones to give me something for the pain? Laud . . . laud . . ."

"Laudanum?"

"That's it. How about it? Damn it, you're the one that did this to me."

Handy said wearily, "All right. I'll talk to him."

He went outside, again locking the door carefully. He was glad of something to do because he didn't want to sit and think. He walked to the Free State Saloon and stepped inside. Instantly the babble of talk quieted.

Doc Bennett was standing at the end of the bar. He had a half-finished drink in front of him. Handy said, "Holloman's in pain. He wants to know if you can give him some laudanum."

Doc Bennett nodded. His worn black bag was on the bar beside him. He picked it up, then as an afterthought finished his drink. He turned, having a little difficulty meeting the sheriff's eyes. He blamed himself for the Indian's death. If he'd come down to Grosbeck's the minute he heard about the Indian being there in chains, he could probably have saved the young man's life.

Pete Handy followed him out of the saloon into the street. Bennett shivered slightly from the chill autumn air. In silence, the pair walked down the boardwalk toward the jail. Halfway there Doc said suddenly, "I'm sorry about the Indian, Pete."

Handy did not reply. Bennett scowled irritably. He felt guilty enough without having Handy condemn him too. He said defensively, "If you'd seen the things I have . . . things those damned Cheyenne have done to settlers and their families . . ."

Handy said, "That's finished, Doc."

"No it isn't. Not by a long sight. That dead Indian will start it all over again. You shouldn't have let Joseph

63

take him back."

Handy didn't answer him. They reached the jail and Handy unlocked the door. Doc went in and Handy followed him back to Sime Holloman's cell. He let Doc into the cell and returned to the office, saying shortly, "Call me when you're through."

He knew Bennett felt guilty about his failure to treat the Indian soon enough to save his life. Grosbeck felt guilty now about letting the Indian be displayed in the window of his store. Karl Spitzer felt guilty about the manacles. The trouble was, guilt wouldn't make them treat other Indians any different. And something was going to have to change. Before there was another Indian war. Before a lot more innocent people were killed.

He paced irritably back and forth until Doc called to him from Holloman's cell. He let Doc out. Bennett said, "I gave Farley some laudanum too. His mouth was hurting him."

Handy blew out the lamp in the jail cell corridor. He let Doc out the front door and locked it behind him. He blew out the lamp on his desk and stretched out, fully dressed, on the office cot.

He stared at the ceiling, thinking of Bird Woman, remembering. When this was over, he thought, he was going to make a visit to the village of Half Yellow Face. He was going to spend a couple of weeks with her.

He closed his eyes but he didn't sleep. The past kept parading before his eyes. He saw Joseph as a little boy playing with the Indian boys. He saw him in Denver, coming home from school with his eye black, his mouth smashed, his clothes bloodied and torn. He remembered being proud because Joseph stoically refused sympathy, refused also to say what the fight had been about. But

64

Handy had known what it was about.

He slept at last. Twice he awakened during the night, once because of a drunken shout outside in the street, once because Sime Holloman groaned and cursed.

He arose at dawn, stretched, unlocked the door and stepped out into the street. He stared toward the north, wondering where Joseph was, wondering if he was safe.

He went back into the jail and began his daily chores. He emptied the slopjars into the outhouse behind the jail. He swept the corridor and the office floor. When the restaurant opened, he got meals for the prisoners and after that he locked the door and went to the restaurant for his own breakfast.

The sun came up and moved across the sky. It was halfway to its zenith when Tom Spitzer came riding into town. The men of the town must have been watching for him because they came hurrying into the street the minute they heard his horse's hoofs. Karl Spitzer came out of the blacksmith's shop, holding a red-hot horseshoe with his tongs. He spoke briefly to Tom, then followed him up the street, still holding the smoking horseshoe. Tom glanced at Pete Handy, standing in the doorway of the jail, but he didn't speak. He pulled his horse to a halt in front of the Free State Saloon.

In spite of the early hour the doors erupted a dozen men. Tony Gallo, wiping his hands on his dirty apron, followed them out through the swinging doors.

Karl Spitzer caught up. Jared Brown came waddling out of the hotel across the street. McDevitt and Grosbeck came running down Main, out of breath but anxious not to miss anything. Brown said, "Well? Well? Are the troopers on the way?"

Tom Spitzer slid wearily from his horse. The men formed a circle around him but he looked at Jared

65

Brown. He handed Brown an envelope.

Brown tore it open. He scanned it, his face growing ever more florid as he did. Someone in the crowd asked, "What's it say? For Christ's sake, what's it say?"

Brown looked up. "It says we're not going to get any troops."

"For God's sake, why not?"

"The commandant says that most of the fort's garrison is out on patrol and not expected back for at least a week. He says he won't strip the fort of the small garrison that's left."

Grosbeck said, "He can't do that. He's got to give us protection from the Indians! That's what them sonsa-bitchin' troopers are out here for."

Handy arrived from the jail. He saw the worry in Grosbeck's face. He saw the same worry in Karl Spitzer and in Doc Bennett. Someone asked fearfully, "What are we gonna do?"

Spitzer said, "We shoulda stopped Joseph. That's what we shoulda done."

"But we didn't. So what do we do now?"

Brown raised his voice. "Shut up, all of you. I'm not through reading this."

"What else does it say?"

"It says we ought to bring the three buffalo hunters to Fort Hays. It says they're willing to hold 'em in the stockade until the circuit judge arrives. The commandant figures if the killers aren't in Indian Wells, the Cheyenne won't attack."

Spitzer looked at Pete Handy. The others turned to look at the sheriff too. Brown asked, "What about it, Pete? You willing to take those three buffalo hunters down to Hays?"

Handy shook his head.

66

"Why not? For Christ's sake, why not?"

Handy said, "We don't even know any Indians are coming here. Holloman's got a bad shoulder wound and Farley's had about four front teeth pulled. There's no use forcing them to make that trip when there probably isn't even any need for it."

"But what if the Cheyenne come?"

Handy frowned. "What if they do? They're not likely to believe that we took the buffalo hunters down to Hays, are they?"

Grosbeck said, "Damn you, you're just tryin' to get even for the Indian."

Handy stared at Grosbeck, his eyes cold and hard and after several moments of trying desperately to meet the sheriff's glance, Grosbeck gave up and looked away, an angry flush mounting into his face.

Brown, obviously trying to break the tension, spoke to Tom Spitzer. "You didn't tell anyone how that Indian died, did you, Tom? You didn't tell 'em about the chains or about Grosbeck's store window or anything?"

Tom looked puzzled. "Why?"

"Never mind why. Did you tell 'em or didn't you?"

"I didn't tell them anything except that the Indian was shot by three buffalo hunters and that he was dead. I told them the buffalo hunters were in jail."

Brown heaved an audible sigh of relief. He looked around at the faces of the men surrounding young Spitzer and his horse. He said, "All of you had better keep quiet about that Indian and you'd better tell your wives to keep quiet too. If the newspapers in Kansas City or St. Louis get hold of the story of the chains and the store window it will set this town back twenty years. You understand?"

There was a murmur of grumbling assent. The men

67

stood there for several moments, as if not knowing what they ought to do. Then, silently and glumly, they dispersed. Brown crossed the street to his hotel, the letter from the Fort Hays commandant a crumpled wad of paper in his hand. Grosbeck and McDevitt walked up Main together. Spitzer and Tom headed for the blacksmith shop. The others went back into the saloon.

Handy remained in the dusty, sun-drenched street for a moment. He was beginning to feel worried now himself. He supposed he had thought troops would be available if they should be needed to protect the town.

He looked wryly inward and discovered that he hadn't really cared whether troops would be available or not. He'd been angry at the people of the town, for their barbarity in permitting the wounded Indian to be displayed. He had also been angry at them for refusing to accept Joseph as one of them. When he let Joseph ride out with the body of the dead Indian he had in reality been getting even with the people of the town.

Admitting that, he wasn't very proud of himself. He had been elected by the people of the county, most of whom lived in Indian Wells, to protect them and keep the peace. He had betrayed their trust. He had placed them in danger for his own satisfaction, to punish them.

Slowly he walked back toward the jail, more troubled than he would have been willing to admit.

CHAPTER 10

IT WAS ALMOST DAWN OF THE FOLLOWING DAY WHEN Joseph reached Indian Wells. He entered the town from the north expecting to find everyone asleep, surprised when they were not. The Free State Saloon was not only open it was full. Down at the jail he could see a dimly burning light.

He was tired all the way to the marrow of his bones. He knew he ought to go to the jail and report what had happened to his father but he wanted a drink before he did. He drew his worn-out horse to a halt in front of the saloon, slid stiffly from the saddle and looped the reins around the rail.

He stumbled crossing the walk toward the swinging doors, recovered and went in. The place quieted almost instantly. He crossed to the bar and the men there made room for him. Joseph looked at Tony Gallo. "Whisky."

Gallo got a bottle and glass and set it in front of him. Down at the end of the bar a drunken buffalo hunter yelled, "Hey. You can't serve whisky to a goddam Indian! It's agin the law!"

Joseph didn't look up. He poured his glass full and drank it in two gulps. It warmed him all the way down. He poured a second. And now he turned his glance toward the buffalo hunter at the end of the bar. He said, "He's serving the white half of me."

Several men laughed uneasily. Joseph returned his attention to the glass in front of him. He stared at it gloomily. The whisky was beginning to take effect. It made him feel dizzy and light-headed. It made him feel like he didn't give a damn. He drank the second one.

69

Talk was beginning again, but around Joseph there was a little island of silence. He could feel the resentful glances of those nearest him. Jared Brown, next to him, asked. "Did you get that dead Indian back to his village all right?"

Joseph turned his head. He nodded.

"No trouble?"

Joseph shrugged. "I'm here and I'm in one piece."

"That isn't answering my question."

Joseph fumbled in his pocket. He found a quarter and laid it on the bar. Tony Gallo gave him change.

Brown said, "Joseph . . ."

Joseph said, "I haven't slept since I left here night before last. Talk to the sheriff." He turned and went out into the faintly graying light of dawn.

It was cold enough to see his breath. He shivered slightly as he untied his horse. He led the animal the half block to the jail and tied him again out front. He glanced at the graying horizon toward the north, wondering how close the five young braves were now.

He went inside. Pete was dozing with his boots up on the desk. He came awake at the sound of the door opening and put his feet down on the floor. He reached over and turned up the lamp, then peered at Joseph with plain relief. "I'm glad you're all right. I was worried."

Joseph staggered as he crossed the room and sank into a chair. Pete studied him several moments before he asked, "How's your mother?"

"She's fine. She was sorry you didn't come."

"Did you find out where the Indian belonged?"

Joseph nodded. "His name was Fat Bear. He belonged in the village of Spotted Horse on Red Willow Creek."

Handy nodded. "I know Spotted Horse. Any

70

trouble?"

"A little. Most of it stirred up by a man named Badger. Know him?"

Pete Handy grinned. "I know him. He wanted your ma and he never forgave me for getting her."

"Well, five young braves chased me until I lost them in the dark. I figure they'll show up outside of town before very long. And if I'm any judge, Badger will show up later with fifty or a hundred more."

Pete nodded without surprise. Joseph said, "You expected that and you still let me go?"

Handy nodded ruefully. "I was mad at the town for letting that boy lie in Grosbeck's window all that time. I guess I was getting back at them. But I didn't think they'd get turned down when they asked for troops." He got up and paced back and forth nervously. "I let my feelings control my judgment. I was wrong."

Joseph sat sprawled in the chair trying hard to stay awake. Handy said, "Go on home and get some sleep. Nothing's likely to happen for a while."

Joseph got wearily to his feet. He tried to smile at Handy but it didn't come off very well. He went out, mounted his horse and rode up Main to the little house they shared on the corner of Main and Elm.

He put his horse into the stable behind the house, unsaddled, and gave him a feed of hay. He had watered him earlier just outside of town. He staggered to the house, went in and sprawled face down across the bed. He was instantly asleep.

Handy, who had followed Joseph out the door, watched him ride up the street toward home. Joseph sat slumped in his saddle, half asleep even as he rode. Handy stared beyond him at the low hills north of town. Joseph had

71

said five young braves chased him out of the village on Red Willow Creek. The five were probably out there in the darkness now, less than half a mile from town.

Five young braves could hardly threaten a town of over a hundred inhabitants. But they might make a hit and run raid at dawn. They might try to set fires at the edge of town. Or they might have reinforcements Joseph didn't know about.

He turned and closed the office door. He locked it. Shivering in the dawn chill, he headed up Main Street toward the Free State Saloon.

Men were leaving when he arrived. He called them back. "Come inside for a minute. I want to talk to you." He went in and faced them, his back to the bar. Gallo poured a drink and pushed it toward him. Handy raised it to his lips and gulped it down. It tasted like hell this time of day. What he needed was coffee. He put down the glass and said, "Five young Indian braves chased Joseph home from Red Willow Creek."

An alarmed murmur went around the room. Handy said, "Five can't hurt us much but they can set fires and they might grab somebody if they get the chance. I'd suggest that you pick eight or ten men to do sentry duty. I'd suggest you do it now because if those Indians make a hit-and-run raid they'll do it in the next half hour or so."

Immediately all the men in the saloon began to talk at once. Handy went out. He untied the first horse he came to and swung to the animal's back. He rode up Main Street toward the northern edge of town, keeping the horse at a steady trot. There was a rifle in the saddle boot and he pulled it out and checked to see that it was loaded. It was.

By the time be reached the upper limit of town, the

72

whole sky was gray. He drew rein and sat there like a statue studying the empty land. He saw nothing but he hadn't expected to. The five young Cheyenne would have tied their horses in a gully someplace out of sight. They'd have crept forward carefully. They might see him but he wouldn't see them until they wanted to be seen.

He heard hoofbeats behind him and turned his head. Grosbeck and Spitzer came galloping up Main, accompanied by a cowhand named Slim and a buffalo hunter Handy didn't know. All were armed. All were shivering slightly with the morning chill.

Both Spitzer and Grosbeck scowled at him. Handy rode away without speaking and began a circle of the town. He went west on Box Elder Street to First and then continued to the alley beyond. He rode down the alley as far as Chestnut Street before he encountered the two men who had been assigned to watch the western edge of town. Both looked scared and jumpy and held their rifles as if they fully expected to have to use them at any time.

Handy continued until he reached Indian Creek. He followed its course in a northeasterly direction past Radinski's Hide Yard. In the middle of Main Street, three more men waited uneasily, staring out across the plain.

At the Chestnut Street bridge across Indian Creek, Handy found two more men. Satisfied that the town was adequately guarded, he headed along Chestnut Street toward Main.

Main Street was utterly deserted. The horses racked outside the Free State Saloon were the only signs of life. Handy dismounted in front of the saloon, tied his borrowed horse and went inside.

Everybody seemed to be talking at once and more men were present than when he had left a little while ago. Some were not even fully dressed, most were unshaven, but all were armed and all were scared.

Sol Radinski saw Handy enter and yelled at him, "You started this! If you hadn't let Joseph take that body back, in this fix we wouldn't be right now. What we want to know is what you're going to do."

Handy looked at him quizzically. "What would you suggest I do?"

"Go out and talk to them. You speak their gibberish."

Handy asked patiently, "What should I tell them, Sol?"

"Tell them . . . Well, you can start by telling them you'll give them the three buffalo hunters if they'll go away."

Handy shook his head.

"Damn you, you got no right to put us all in danger just to save them three murderers!"

The word "right" triggered something explosive in Pete Handy's mind. He faced Radinski, coldly furious. "Don't you talk to me about right! You people don't have the first notion of what is right! You want to blame me and you want to blame Joseph for starting this trouble but if a single one of you had done what he should have that Indian wouldn't be dead and the town wouldn't be in this stinking fix!"

Radinski's face turned pale. Doc Bennett kept trying to meet the sheriff's glance but he couldn't manage it. Finally he gave up and stared steadily at the floor between his feet.

Handy was so angry his hands were trembling. He fixed his glance on Doc. "If anyone's to blame for what's happening, it's you! You could have saved him

74

if you'd treated him the same day the buffalo hunters brought him in. But no, by God! You'd seen too many atrocities, hadn't you? But had you ever seen an atrocity committed by that eighteen-year-old Indian boy?"

Doc glanced up miserably. He didn't even try to defend himself. His guilt was plain in his face and Handy knew suddenly that nothing he could say to Doc would be as bad as what Doc was saying to himself.

He let his furious glance sweep the crowd in the saloon. "Not a goddam one of you is clean. All of you stood on the sidewalk in front of Grosbeck's and stared in through the window at him. All of you saw his wounds. All of you knew that if he didn't get help he was going to die. But none of you did a goddam thing."

A big, dirty, bearded buffalo hunter growled, "He wasn't nothin' but a goddam animal. Why all the fuss over him? I got more use for my dog than I have for a Indian."

Handy shifted his glance, his eyes hard and cold and furious. He said, "Mister, I married an Indian. You want to tell me my wife is nothing but an animal?"

The man looked trapped and cornered but his expression said he knew he couldn't back down now. He growled, "Hell yes, I'm telling you. Crawlin' into bed with a animal don't make her human. Not by a damsite. Not by a damsite, by God, not . . ." His voice trailed off. His eyes, resting on Handy's face, widened. His hand strayed toward his holstered gun.

Handy's voice was like a whip. "Touch it and you're dead!"

The man let his hand fall away. Men were scattering now, to right and left, crowding each other frantically. The buffalo hunter was left alone at the bar, alone to face Pete Handy's white-faced wrath. He glanced to right and left as though looking for support. There was none. He started to open his mouth, then closed it again.

He pushed himself away from the bar. He knew he had to fight. He knew there was no way out.

Handy began a slow, deliberate advance, more furious than he had ever been in his life before. He wanted to kill, but not with a gun. He wanted to kill this man with his two bare hands.

CHAPTER 11

THE HUNTER WAS TALLER THAN HANDY, RANGY AND loose but he weighed about the same. He moved with ease and economy and now, after shifting his position only slightly, waited for Handy, his eyes wary and watchful and intent. His expression said he knew this was an encounter he had no chance to win. If he beat the sheriff with his fists he would be guilty of assault and would have to get out of town or go to jail. If he lost, be would probably wake up in jail.

He forced Handy to come to him, forced the sheriff to make the first attack. He didn't regret what he'd said about Indians. That was his opinion and he figured he was entitled to it. But he wouldn't have included Handy's wife unless Handy had forced him to.

In his opinion, a squaw was a squaw, not to be put into a class with white women. Not even in the same class with saloon white women or with those who stood at the windows of the brothels down the street.

Handy feinted with lightning speed for a man so big and the buffalo hunter moved to meet the feint. Too late, he saw he had been taken in because Handy wasn't there. He swung wildly, missing, by the violence of his

76

swing whirling himself halfway around. Something exploded in his brain and the whole right side of his head turned numb. He was flung back against the bar so hard that he rocked the thing on its base, tore nails out and sent glasses and bottles cascading to the floor.

Pete Handy felt his fist slam into the rock-hard side of the hunter's head with a shock he felt all the way to his shoulder. He followed that first blow with another that caught the hunter still slumped against the bar. This one snapped his head back hard enough to make his neck crack audibly.

A hoarse voice yelled, "Hey!" and the hunter's companion came at Handy from the side, rifle upraised like a club. Handy swung his head, eyes bloodshot with his fury, his mouth a gash in his taut-muscled face.

The hunter had time to wish he'd stayed out of this, then swung the rifle in a last, frantic attempt to save himself. Handy caught it coming down, caught its awful force in his two broad hands. They gave before it but they had an iron grip on it. He wrenched it away and threw it savagely toward the door.

It missed the door, hit a window instead and took out both glass and window sash as it went through. It fell in the dusty street beyond the boardwalk and skidded half a dozen feet before it stopped.

Handy caught the second buffalo hunter's beard and yanked the man violently toward him. The hunter plunged forward, hopelessly off balance, and Handy stepped aside, letting the man's head slam into the heavy bar. Again it gave and rocked, and again glasses and bottles cascaded to the floor. The second hunter, unconscious, slid to the floor at Handy's feet.

The first one was recovering. He struggled into an upright position, temporarily supporting himself by hooking his elbows on the bar in back of him. He glared owlishly at Handy, trying to focus his eyes, trying to grasp his fading consciousness and hold to it. He mumbled, "You goddam sonofabitch! I'll . . ."

Handy sank a fist into his belly and when he doubled forward, let him have it squarely in the face.

The hunter knew he was beat but there was a stubbornness in him that wouldn't let him go down without trying everything. He grabbed his gun out of its holster, too furious to realize be might be provoking the already thoroughly provoked sheriff to kill him then and there.

But Handy had control of himself by now. His first fury at the hunter's remarks had spent itself and he was sane enough to realize that when he struck out at the hunter he was in reality striking out at everyone in town, at everyone who had stared through Grosbeck's window at the wounded Indian, at everyone who had made living here hard for Joseph, at everyone here and elsewhere who made it impossible for him to have Bird Woman with him all the time.

The hunter, stunned, was slow getting out his gun and there was no need for Handy to use his own gun to defend himself. He seized the hunter's wrist with one hand, his elbow with the other, and brought the arm down against his rising knee.

The gun clattered to the floor. The hunter howled with pain. Handy didn't know whether he'd broken the man's arm or not. He didn't care. He let the hunter slide, half-conscious, to the floor, then turned to glare murderously at the men huddled against the walls. His glance dared them to intervene.

Jared Brown was the first to move. He came forward, followed by Doc Bennett, who immediately knelt at the buffalo hunter's side. He picked the man's arm up carefully and Handy said bitterly, "It's too bad you didn't show a little of the same concern for that wounded Indian."

Doc did not look up. Jared Brown said, "You had no call to half kill these two."

Handy suddenly felt very tired. He stared at Brown and at the others who were now returning to the bar. He didn't intend to argue with them and he didn't intend to justify himself.

Brown said, "You're not going to jail them, are you?"

Handy shook his head. "I've got too many in jail right now. Just tell them to keep out of my way."

Someone, somewhere, said, "Who the hell does he think be is?"

Ignoring that, Handy turned and tramped to the swinging doors. He slammed them open with such force that they banged noisily against the outside of the building. Behind him, he heard Jared Brown say, "Well, we voted for him. Now we're stuck with him."

Another voice said, "Jesus! He didn't have to be that rough. All that hunter said was . . . ."

He was too far away to understand the rest of it, not too far to hear the murmur of grumbling. He went on to the jail, sourly angry but ashamed of himself as well. He *had* been unnecessarily rough with the buffalo hunters. He'd had no right to beat them up for no more than saying what they thought.

He unlocked the door of the jail and started to step inside. Remembering the Indians, he turned and stared up the street, then down it past the hide yard and the livery stable across from it. He saw nothing, which surprised him not at all. He doubted if there were enough Indians out there to give Indian Wells any

79

trouble today even if reinforcements had arrived.

He went in and closed the door. He heard a yell from back in the cells. "Hey, Sheriff! What the hell's all the commotion out there in the street? What's going on?"

Handy didn't see any reason to evade. The prisoners had just as well know what was going on. He went back into the corridor between the cells. He said, "Five Indian braves chased Joseph home from the village where he took that dead Indian for burial. They're outside of town right now. The townspeople have been posting sentries to see that they don't grab anyone or set fire to any buildings."

"What do they want? Joseph?"

"Maybe they want him now. They'll likely end up wanting you."

"Why? Did he tell them we killed the Indian?"

"He told them."

Holloman said, "You don't intend for us to go to trial. You know goddam good and well that there ain't a jury in the whole state of Kansas that would convict us of killing that Indian."

"I don't know about that. But you're going to trial all right."

"What if more Indians show up? They're liable to."

"I'll worry about that when they do."

"You'd better worry about it now. Have you sent to Hays for troops?"

Handy said, "The mayor did."

"When will they get here?"

"They won't. The commandant said his troops were all out on patrol and wouldn't be back for at least a week."

"Then you'd better send us down to Hays."

Handy shook his head.

Luke Kitchen spoke up, his voice thin and scared. "What about me, Pete? How about letting me out until this is over with?"

"I can't."

"I got a right to be out on bail."

"Not unless the judge sets bail and there's damn seldom any bail in murder cases. You know that much."

"What do you think they'll do to me? I didn't mean to kill that guy. It was just a fight. Besides, I thought he had a gun. I was so goddam drunk and mad . . ."

"I guess the judge will take that into account. But don't get to figurin' you're going to get off. You'll probably get at least two years."

"Oh Jesus! Two years! How in hell will I stand two years cooped up like an animal?" He glanced quickly at the sheriff as though his words had suddenly rung a bell somewhere in his mind.

Holloman got up from the bunk and came across to the bars. His face turned white from the pain in his shoulder. Beads of sweat sprang out on his forehead and upper lip. He asked, "You've got a reason for not wanting to send us to Fort Hays, haven't you?"

"Reason?"

"Sure. You figure that if the goin' gets too rough, you can just turn us over to the Indians."

Pete Handy grinned sourly, "That's not as bad an idea as you think. It might save the town from an Indian attack."

Holloman stared at him incredulously.

Handy said, "Besides, sending you to Fort Hays is riskier than you think. There are five young Indian braves out there itching to kill a white man—any white man. I'd have to send you under heavy guard and I don't have the men for it."

81

"How about some of the townspeople?"

Handy asked, "Who, for instance? Do you know any of the townspeople who would risk their necks for the likes of you?"

"They don't mind takin' our money when we come in with our hides."

"So in return you think they ought to risk their lives for you?" He paused. "Why should they? It was you who brought the trouble to the town. You're the ones that shot the Indian. You had the irons put on him and you put him in the window of the hardware store. Right now, it would be my guess that the townspeople don't feel too damn friendly toward you."

"It wasn't us that brought them five Indians here. It was your goddam half-breed son. He didn't have to take that stinking Indian home the way he did. You could have buried him right here."

Handy nodded. "I suppose we could. But we didn't."

"And now we have to pay the price for your stupidity. What if the whole Cheyenne tribe takes a notion to attack the town?"

"You'd better hope they don't because it would sure as hell put a strain on my sense of duty. I'd get to weighing the lives of the townspeople against your three worthless hides. It might not work out too well for you."

Holloman scowled. Farley and Weigand stared sullenly at him from their bunks.

Handy turned and went back into his office. He sat down and put his feet up on the desk. He wasn't worried about being taken by surprise. There were armed sentries on the edge of town. If any Indians showed themselves the gunshots of the sentries would alert him soon enough.

He found his pipe and tobacco and packed the pipe.

He put it into his mouth, lighted it and puffed thoughtfully. What would he do if a large force of Indians attacked, he wondered. What *could* he do?

He couldn't do much, he admitted. He and Joseph could fight with the townspeople and that was all.

He got up and began to pace back and forth, puffing the pipe furiously. He'd gotten the town into this. It was up to him to figure a way of getting it out again.

CHAPTER 12

A BREEZE BLOWING FROM THE SOUTH CARRIED THE stink of the hide yard up Main and into the saloon. The sun was up and the shadow of the saloon laid on the dusty street, reaching almost to the veranda of the Brown Hotel across from it. Out on the prairie north of town a coyote barked, to be answered by another, and by still another.

The sounds weren't heard inside the Free State Saloon. There was too much talk. Jared Brown stared around at the excited men. He was florid of face and his body was flabby but there was an inner toughness to him that became apparent under stress.

He could understand the hatred toward Indians felt by almost everybody in Indian Wells. Hardly a one of them had escaped being touched by the Indians' barbarity. Yet he knew the town's barbarity in permitting the wounded Indian to be displayed in chains had equaled any barbarity shown settlers in and around Indian Wells by the Indians.

There was a little, nagging feeling of guilt in the back of his own mind whenever he thought of it. In the sheriff's absence, he was the one who should have put a stop to it. He should have done what Handy had and forced Doc Bennett to treat the Indian. He should have made Karl Spitzer remove the manacles. He should have lodged the Indian in a cell down at the jail and, by so doing, given him a chance to live.

Perhaps the Indian would have died anyway. Brown took refuge in that thought. Yet he knew it was a false refuge. It didn't matter whether the Indian would have died. What did matter was that he, like everyone else in town, had allowed the young Cheyenne to lie, untended and in great pain, in Grosbeck's store window for three long days.

He listened to the talk with only a part of his mind.

Most of the townsmen were now blaming Holloman and Farley and Weigand for shooting the Indian and bringing him, wounded, into town.

Over in the corner a bitter argument raged between some townsmen and some buffalo hunters. A hunter named Rhodes angrily shouted the townsmen down. His gray beard was stained with tobacco juice. His close-set eyes were blazing furiously as he shouted, "Hypocrites! You thought that Indian was a damn fine show. Grosbeck said it was good for business. Said people were stopping to look in his store window for the first time in months. Said his sales had doubled and maybe he ought to keep an Indian in there all the time. Now you want to lay the blame on Holloman and Farley and Weigand."

Sol Radinski bawled angrily, "It wouldn't have happened if they hadn't brought him into town! It was their idea to put manacles on him and put him in the window of the hardware store. Now look what's happening! There's wild Indians right outside of town. Hunters won't dare bring their hides into Indian Wells."

84

Rhodes stared at Radinski contemptuously. "You sonofabitch! That's what's worrying you, isn't it? Your lousy goddam hide business!"

Brown shouted, "Quiet. Quiet all of you. Calling names isn't going to solve anything. This town is in a fix and it isn't just the Indians outside of town."

The argument stopped. Brown's voice had the ring of authority. He said, "First of all, we'd better make sure the Indians don't destroy the town. All of you had better go home and arm yourselves. And bring your women and children down to the hotel."

The men stared at him worriedly. Radinski asked, "Do you think there is going to be a real uprising, Mr. Brown?"

"I think we'd better be ready in case there is."

"You said it wasn't just the Indians outside of town. What else is there?"

"We'd better make sure the story of that Indian don't leak out. The stage is due today. I don't know if it's going to get through the Indians but if it does, keep it in mind that it's going East. Don't tell any of the passengers about the Indian. If there should be an uprising and if the story gets into the newspapers—hell, there's no telling what the consequences could be. The Indian Bureau might bring federal charges against all of us, against Grosbeck and Spitzer, and Doc and me. And even if they don't you know what the story will do to Indian Wells."

There was silence in the place as the men considered what he had said. Brown shouted, "All right. Go home and get your guns. Bring your families and you'd each better bring along whatever food you can. We might be holed up in the hotel for several days."

Bennett asked, "How are you going to explain every-

85

body being holed up in the hotel to the stage passengers?" Brown frowned at him. "We don't have to explain anything. They'll know there are Indians around by the time the coach rolls into town. And that's all they need to know."

The men began to leave. In less than two minutes the place was empty except for seven buffalo hunters, two of whom were the ones Handy had beaten so thoroughly, and three cowhands. Tony Gallo dug his shotgun out from underneath the bar. He loaded it and placed it on top of the bar along with a box of shells. Nervously he began to mop the bar with his dirty rag.

Rhodes stood at the swinging doors, staring over them into the street. He turned his head and glanced at Brown. "If you had any sense you'd send a dozen or so men out to get those Indians. It'd sure discourage any more that happened to show up."

Brown said, "Or make matters worse." He picked up his glass and gulped his drink. He didn't usually drink this early in the day but then he wasn't usually subjected to this kind of stress.

He went outside and stood for a moment on the walk, staring uneasily up and down as if half expecting to see Indians. When he didn't, he crossed the street and climbed the four steps to the veranda of the hotel.

Radinski wasn't the only one who benefitted from the buffalo hunters coming here, he thought. He also did and maybe that was one reason he hadn't made any fuss about the wounded Indian. He hadn't wanted to antagonize them. Buffalo hunters, after spending six months out on the prairie sleeping on the ground, usually wanted an honest-to-God bed more than anything when they hit town. He grinned faintly to himself as he glanced toward the brothels down the street. More than almost anything, he amended. And a man didn't antagonize those who provided his livelihood. Not if he had any sense.

He went into the lobby. Davey Locke was standing at the window, looking out. No one else was there. Davey asked, "Do you think the stage will get through, Mr. Brown?"

"I don't know," Brown said. "Anyway, we've got better things to think about. Everybody in town is coming here until this Indian scare is over with. Go check the vacant rooms and see if they're ready. Tell Mrs. Weisbart what's happening and tell her she may have a hundred people here for dinner at noon."

Davey, who was sixteen, headed for the kitchen excitedly. Brown could hear him talking to Mrs. Weisbart the minute he opened the door. He grinned faintly, thinking what her response would be. She'd complain bitterly but when noon came there would be food for a hundred people in the dining room.

He began to pace nervously back and forth across the white-tile lobby floor, occasionally pausing at the window to look out into the deserted street.

Pete Handy stepped out of the jail when he saw the exodus begin at the Free State Saloon. There was approval in his eyes as he saw the townsmen hurrying toward their homes. He'd have mobilized the townsmen himself later in the day but it suited him that Brown had done it first.

He turned and walked to the livery stable. Lew Gavin, who owned the stable, was approaching from the saloon. A bachelor, Gavin slept in the stable tackroom and took all his meals at McDevitt's Restaurant. When Gavin reached the stable Handy said, "Get my horse," and waited while Gavin led his horse up front and saddled him. Gavin offered no comment. He just stared sullenly as the sheriff mounted and rode out of the livery barn into the street.

Indian Creek ran past the livery stable on the south. Handy rode into its bed, then east through old town and its original sod buildings, most of them now crumbling with age and neglect. Beyond Second Avenue Indian Creek turned north, not again veering east until it had passed beneath the Chestnut Street bridge.

Two men were on the bridge. Their horses were tied to the bridge rail. Both were smoking pipes and both seemed more relaxed than when Handy had seen them last. He stopped long enough to ask, "Seen anything?"

Ben Thompson, who did the gunsmithing for Grosbeck, shook his head. A coyote yipped on the prairie east of town, to be answered by another one. Handy stared toward the sounds, seeing nothing. Thompson asked, "Indians?" and Handy nodded. Both Thompson and the other man, a buffalo hunter Handy didn't know by name, looked worriedly toward the empty prairie from which the sounds had come. Handy said, "I doubt if anything's going to happen for a while but keep your eyes open anyway."

"Don't worry," Ben Thompson said. "Just knowin' those sneaky devils are out there is enough to keep me on the job."

Handy went on, still staying in the bed of the creek. When he reached Box Elder Street, the last on the north side of town, he climbed his horse out and rode down the middle of the street.

Grosbeck and Spitzer were no longer on sentry duty with Slim and the buffalo hunter. Handy asked where they were.

"They went home to get their families and take them down to the hotel. The mayor wants everybody there."

"Are they coming back?"

"They said they were."

"Seen anything?"

"No, but there's a hell of a lot of coyotes out there."

"Indians. Signaling." Handy grinned. "Or just trying to make you boys nervous. Don't let them get your goats. When there are enough of them to give the town trouble you won't hear them. You'll see them."

The buffalo hunter was young, redheaded, and scared. His first year hunting buffalo, Handy thought. The Indian who had died in Grosbeck's window was probably the first wild Indian he had ever seen.

He rode on, west now along Box Elder Street. Where it crossed Main he saw Will Thornhill leading his family into a buggy, along with whatever valuables they could carry in their arms. He nodded and received only cold, hostile stares from Thornhill and his wife.

He went on to the alley west of First Avenue. The two men, Klaas and Montoya, who had been assigned to guard the western edge of town watched him approach. When he was close enough they asked in unison, "What's going on?"

"Jared Brown wants everybody to bring their families to the hotel. I'll see that you get relieved long enough to do it. Seen anything?"

Martin Klaas, who clerked in the Kansas Mercantile, pointed a stubby finger toward the northwest. "We saw some Indians on that ridge a while ago."

"How many? How were they dressed?"

"Six or eight I guess. They had on them fancy headdresses. You know—with all the feathers and everything. One had a couple of buffalo horns stickin' out of it."

Handy nodded, keeping his face expressionless. "Let me know if you see anything else. I'll send a couple of men out to relieve you right away."

He rode south along the alley, now frowning worriedly. The young braves who had chased Joseph back to town wouldn't have been wearing more than a feather or two in their hair. Six or eight silhouetted on the ridge with ceremonial headdresses meant that the young braves had been reinforced.

He rounded Radinski's Hide Yard and rode up Main to the hotel. A dozen rigs were tied in front. There were at least a dozen horses racked in front of the hotel and in front of the saloon across the street. Jared Brown stood on the hotel veranda, shouting to the people to come on in. His hands were on his hips. His legs were spread. Handy grinned faintly to himself.

He rode as close as he could and called, "Klaas and Montoya want you to relieve them so they can get their families."

Brown called out to a couple of men to relieve the two. They rode away toward the western edge of town. Handy headed up Main toward his own small house on Elm. He tied his horse and went in. He could hear Joseph snoring and hated to awaken him but he knew he had no choice. Joseph could sleep down at the jail if he wanted to. He went into the bedroom and shook Joseph's shoulder. Joseph came awake quickly and silently, the way he always did. Handy said, "Come down to the jail."

"What's happening?"

"Jared Brown is assembling everyone at the hotel. There are more Indians out there now."

"How many?"

90

"I don't know. Martin Klaas and Primitivo Montoya saw six or eight riding along a ridge. They had feathered headdresses on."

Joseph sat up and reached for his rifle. He stood up. "I'll saddle up my horse."

Handy nodded. He went out the front door, mounted and rode down Main toward the jail.

CHAPTER 13

HANDY UNLOCKED THE DOOR OF THE JAIL AND WENT inside. Holloman started yelling but Handy only yelled back irritably, telling him to shut up. He was beginning to feel worried about the safety of the town and he wished the commandant at Fort Hays had been able to send troops.

Joseph rode down the street and stopped in front of the jail. He dismounted and tied his horse. He came inside, "I guess I was pretty stupid for insisting on taking Fat Bear home for burial."

Handy grinned at him ruefully. "I was pretty stupid for letting you. I guess we both were trying to get even and I guess getting even is a luxury a lawman can't afford." He didn't tell Joseph but he had already decided that when this was over there would be but one course open to him. He would have to resign.

"What are you going to do?" Joseph asked.

"I'm going over to the hotel. After that, I'm going to ride out and have a talk with the Indians."

"You can't talk to them. They'd kill you before you got the chance."

"Huh uh. They're as curious as anybody else. They're not likely to kill me before they hear what I have to

91

say."

"I wish you'd let me go. It's my fault they're there."

"You stay and watch the prisoners. Some of the men might try to get them out and turn them over to the Indians."

He went out, untied his horse and mounted. He rode up the street to the hotel. A crowd of men stood in front of it. Handy stopped and asked, "Where's Brown?"

"Inside."

"Get him. I want to talk to him."

The man he had spoken to looked at him sullenly a moment, then turned and went into the lobby of the hotel. After several moments Brown came out. He looked at Handy questioningly.

Handy said, "I'm going to ride out and talk to the Indians. I'd suggest you get a force of maybe twenty of your best men together and keep them near their horses ready to head off an Indian attack wherever it develops."

Brown nodded agreement. Handy said, "And keep the rest here to defend the hotel."

Again Brown nodded. His expression said he blamed Handy for letting this situation develop. Handy scowled, turned his horse and rode north up Main.

He stopped at the edge of town, scanning the horizon. Suddenly on a ridge to the northwest a score of mounted Indians appeared. They came over the crest of the ridge and stopped skylined there, plumes fluttering in the breeze.

Handy touched spurs to his horse's sides and rode toward them at a steady trot. They were half a mile away, too far for him to recognize individuals but from their headdresses he guessed they were the village elders and headmen. Spotted Horse was undoubtedly among them. Handy was also certain that behind the ridge, hidden from his sight, were other warriors, probably two or three times the number now visible. The young Indians who had pursued Joseph home were nowhere to be seen.

When he was two hundred yards from the top of the ridge, forty or fifty mounted braves suddenly galloped into sight, both on the right and left of the line of headmen facing him. In a couple of minutes they had surrounded him. Several made threatening gestures but he paid no attention to them.

He now could recognize Spotted Horse. He changed course slightly and rode straight to the chief. He raised a hand in the universal sign of peace.

Spotted Horse did not move. Speaking fluently in the Cheyenne tongue, Handy said, "I am Pete Handy, sheriff of this county. I once lived in the village of Half Yellow Face, and I am the husband of Bird Woman, who lives there now."

The young braves were still galloping back and forth. Occasionally one would yell or make a dummy run at Handy with a lance. Spotted Horse's voice roared at them to be still while their elders talked. There was instant silence where before had been only confusion.

Spotted Horse turned to Handy. "Fat Bear was killed by three buffalo hunters who are now in your village. Your son, Joseph, said that they were in jail."

"That is so."

"He said they would be tried for killing Fat Bear but he did not say they would be punished for their crime."

"The court will decide the punishment."

"In our village we might not punish a man who had killed a white."

"And our court might not punish the three who killed

Fat Bear."

Spotted Horse scowled. There was paint on the faces of the village headmen and on that of Spotted Horse. It was war paint, carefully applied. Handy thought that the paint gave them barbaric and rather splendid appearance, but it had the additional effect of making them seem more inscrutable. Spotted Horse said, "You will give the three buffalo hunters to us. We will decide their punishment."

This was what Handy had expected. He had been prepared for it. He said, "And if I don't?"

"Then we will take them from you. We will set fire to your village and we will kill all those who resist."

Handy said, "I am a lawman like one of your dog soldiers who enforce order in your villages. I am not the chief. This is a matter only the chief can decide."

"Then return and tell him what I have said. You have until tomorrow. If I do not have your answer when the sun comes up, we will attack and burn your village. My young men are angry and difficult to control. They have many grievances against the whites. There is no way for me to tell what they may do in the excitement of the attack."

Handy nodded ruefully. He knew the chief's words were not an idle threat. He said, "You will have your answer by the time the sun comes out of the plain tomorrow."

He waited a moment to be sure Spotted Horse had said everything he had to say. Then he turned and rode at a slow walk back toward the town of Indian Wells. He half expected a bullet, an arrow or lance in the back, but nothing happened. When he glanced around, halfway down the slope, the Indians had disappeared.

He continued to the edge of town. A dozen men

94

galloped from the hotel and clustered around him excitedly. "What'd they say? Jesus, there's a hell of a lot of Indians out there. Must've been sixty or seventy!"

. Handy said, "They want the prisoners. The three who killed the Indian."

"Then give 'em up. Three killers ain't worth gettin' the town burned for."

Handy rode through them and trotted his horse toward the hotel. Joseph came to the door of the jail and Handy stopped long enough to say, "Spotted Horse. He wants the hunters who killed Fat Bear."

"Are you going to give them up?"

Handy said, "You know I can't give them up."

"Then what are you going to do?"

Handy shrugged. "I don't know." He rode on up the street to the hotel. It looked like everybody in town was either on the hotel veranda or on the walk in front of it. Brown, Radinski, Grosbeck, Spitzer, and Doc Bennett stood in a group and it was in front of these five that Handy stopped.

Brown asked, "Well? What did they want?"

"The three hunters who killed the Indian."

There was an immediate look of relief on Brown's face. "Well, that's easy. All we've got to do is give them up and the Indians will go away."

A buffalo hunter standing nearby yelled, "Wait a goddam minute! You can't give three white men to those red savages!"

Immediately there was a hubbub of voices. Everybody seemed to be trying to talk at once. Handy waited, letting them argue. He hadn't expected support from the buffalo hunters but he was glad to get any support he could. It meant he wouldn't have to buck the whole town by himself.

Brown's face was red. He raised his hands ineffectively and yelled for quiet. Nobody seemed to hear. Brown shouted louder at them, then shouted even louder when they still didn't hear. After that he waited, fuming, until the discussion quieted spontaneously. At last, when he could be heard, he yelled, "If we don't give them up, the Indians will come after them. That's what the sheriff said." Handy hadn't said that but he didn't dispute the mayor's words. Brown shouted, "Chances are Holloman and Parley and Weigand are going to be found guilty anyhow. They'll either be executed or sent to prison. It don't make a hell of a lot of difference as far as they're concerned whether we give 'em up or not. But it sure makes a difference to the town. There must be close to a hundred Indians out there. By tonight there might be a hundred more." He looked at Handy. "How long do we have to make up our minds?"

"We have today. Spotted Horse said that if he didn't have the three by sunup tomorrow he'd attack the town."

Brown said, "Pete, for God's sake!"

"Jared, you know I can't give up prisoners. Not to the Indians. Not to anyone."

"But the town! Isn't the town more important than three individuals?"

"They've got to go to trial."

"Why? They're guilty. They've admitted their guilt. They admitted they shot that Indian."

Handy glanced at Doc Bennett, at Grosbeck and Spitzer. "They shot him but did they kill him? He might have lived if he'd had the right kind of care."

"They're the ones who had the irons put on. They're the ones who put him in Grosbeck's window."

96

"Spitzer could have refused to put on the irons. Grosbeck could have refused to have him in the window of his store. Bennett could have treated him. And you could have stopped the whole damn thing."

Brown stared at him angrily. "So that's it! You're out to get us, aren't you? You're sore because the town never accepted your half-breed son. And now you figure you've got your chance. You can raise enough stink with this to force the Indian Bureau to bring charges against us in the Indian's death. You can kick up enough fuss to get the whole thing in the newspapers. You can ruin the town and that's what you really want!"

Handy stared at him. "Because I won't turn three prisoners over to be murdered by the Indians?"

"Oh you can hide behind your badge! You can pretend you're just doing your duty, can't you? But we both know better. The whole town knows better!"

Handy looked at Doc. "Is that what you think?"

"I don't know what I think."

"You've been screaming about all the Indian atrocities you've seen. Do you want those hunters turned over to the Indians?"

Doc started to speak, then closed his mouth. He tried to meet Handy's glance and failed.

Handy said a single, obscene word. He turned his horse and rode back toward the jail. For once, there was nothing but silence behind him. It lasted until he reached the jail. Then everybody began to talk at once. The result was a low, ominous-sounding roar.

CHAPTER 14

IT WAS GETTING CLOSE TO NOON. HANDY WENT INTO the jail and sailed his hat disgustedly at his desk. Joseph was studying his face. Handy glanced at him. "Want to go up and get dinner for the prisoners?"

Joseph nodded. He hesitated a moment, then went out into the street. He couldn't help glancing up Main toward the prairie north of town, but he didn't see any Indians.

He tried not to look defiant as he passed the crowd gathered in front of the Free State Saloon but he knew he hadn't brought it off. The silence lasted until he was across the street. Then the talk began again.

Martin Klaas was standing in the doorway of the Kansas Mercantile. He ducked back out of sight when he saw Joseph so he wouldn't have to speak. Joseph frowned. The trouble was, he never got used to being snubbed. You didn't have to like someone to be hurt when they avoided you.

He crossed the street and went into the restaurant. The air was rich with the smell of cooking food. No one was in the place but Joseph could hear pots banging and dishes being handled in the kitchen.

He let the door slam behind him and a moment later Oralee McDevitt came from the kitchen.

Her face was flushed and shining with perspiration. For an instant she looked panicky, as though she wanted to turn and run. Then, getting control of herself, she crossed the room. "Hello, Joseph."

"Hello, Oralee." There was stiffness in both greetings and Oralee would not look at him. He started to tell her

98

he wanted meals for the prisoners, but then stopped. There was no use avoiding the issue between them any longer. The prisoners could wait. He said, "I want to talk to you."

"I'm busy, Joseph. We're getting ready for the dinner rush, I . . ."

"Nobody is here yet. You're not so busy you can't take a few minutes to talk to me."

"What about?"

"About you and me."

"What about us, Joseph?"

He stared at her irritably. "Don't pretend that nothing's wrong."

"Joseph . . ." She looked up now, both fright and determination in her eyes. "Mama and Papa say I have to stop seeing you."

"Because I'm an Indian?"

She nodded.

"And what do you say?"

"Please, Joseph. Please don't make it any harder for me than it already is."

"Why not?" There was anger in him now. "Why should I worry about whether it's hard for you or not? You're telling me you're not going to see me again because I'm an Indian. Don't you think that's a little hard for me to take?"

"I'm sorry, Joseph. I really am. I'm terribly sorry."

"What else did they say?"

A flush crept up into her face. She looked steadily at the floor.

Joseph said bitterly, "Don't answer that. Let me guess. They told you that if you married me all your children would be red Indians, didn't they? They told you they would be treated the way I've always been

99

treated here. They told you your children's children would be Indians, and their children after them."

Oralee didn't look up. Joseph asked harshly. "Didn't they?"

She nodded dumbly.

He stared at her. He had thought he loved her and maybe he had. He still felt a strong desire to take her in his arms, to feel her softness and her warmth. But suddenly, today, he was realizing something he had never realized before. There was no real strength in Oralee. She was pretty and pleasant and he enjoyed her company, but there was no strength in her.

And for the first time he knew something else. He needed a woman who was strong. Only a strong woman could take being treated the way his wife would be treated wherever she lived, wherever she went. Only a strong woman could take it without breaking, without turning bitter, without blaming him.

He realized that, but something in him would not give up. Not so quickly. Not so easily. He said gently, "We'll talk about it some other time. Right now I have to get meals for the prisoners."

He forced a grin. "Four is all. We haven't arrested anybody since breakfast."

She turned and fled to the kitchen, her relief apparent in every line of her body. He pulled out a chair and straddled it, leaning his arms on its back.

A kind of sadness touched him because he now understood better than ever before how hard it had been for his father to leave his mother, how hard it had been for him to live away from her still loving her as he did.

His father had done it for him, and his intentions had been the best. But had it been the right thing to do, either for his son or for himself?

Frowning, Joseph stared out the window into the empty street. He could imagine he heard the soft, diffident tones of John McDevitt talking against him to Oralee, the shriller tones of Oralee's mother chiming in. McDevitt was like Oralee in that he had no strength. He would never face Joseph and tell him to stay away from Oralee. He would leave that unpleasant chore for her to do herself.

He had probably told Oralee, too, that eventually Joseph would take her back to the Indian villages where she would have to live in a hide tipi, where she would have to skin buffalo, and cut up meat, and cure it, and sleep beneath hairy robes and be cold in winter and hot in summer and without a doctor when the time for bearing her children came.

He had frightened her thoroughly, frightened her enough so that she was able to tell Joseph that she couldn't see him any more. Yet she still had lacked the courage to broach the subject to him herself. He'd had to bring it up.

She came from the kitchen carrying two trays and returned for the other two. When she came back with them Joseph said, "Help me carry them." He didn't want to leave her yet. Not with things the way they were.

She nodded. He picked up two of the trays and carried them to the door. He held it open while Oralee went through. She headed toward the jail and he followed close behind.

Her back was straight and slim and her head was high.

Her hips moved as she walked and suddenly there was a kind of ache in him because he knew that now he could never hold her in the night, could never look at

101

her across the breakfast table, could never hold her fiercely gripping hands while she gave birth. Not because he was not a good and decent man either, but because he was half Indian, because there was a different color to his skin.

She walked swiftly and he kept up with her. In front of the Free State Saloon men stepped aside to give her the walk. They looked at Joseph with smoldering anger as he passed.

Pete Handy held the door open while they carried the trays into the jail. Joseph put his two trays on the desk and took Oralee's from her. Handy looked first at Oralee and then at Joseph. He said, "I'll take them to the prisoners. You walk Oralee back." It was plain that he had seen the tension between the two. It was also plain that he had guessed its cause.

Going out with Oralee, Joseph wondered why he didn't just leave Indian Wells and go back to the village of Half Yellow Face. He could find an Indian girl and marry her. He could, at least, be accepted. He could be part of his environment, one of those among whom he lived.

Oralee seemed anxious to get away from him but be caught her and gripped her arm. He could feel a rapid pulse beating in it. He could see how pale she was. He realized with a shock that she was afraid of him.

He released her immediately. He said, "You've known me a long, long time. You know there's no reason to be afraid of me."

"I'm not . . ." She looked up at him. "No. That isn't true. I guess I am afraid of you."

"Why? I'm no different."

"No. I suppose you're not. It's me. Your Indian blood . . . I mean, maybe I never really knew you at all."

He said bitterly, "You make it sound like I was half grizzly bear."

"Oh Joseph," she said impatiently. "You're turning my words around."

He said, "You won't believe this, but Indians are human. They laugh when they're happy and they cry when they're sad and they bleed when they're hurt."

"Joseph, there are a million miles between us."

They were nearing the crowd of men in front of the saloon. Joseph didn't reply because he didn't want to be overheard. He crossed the street with Oralee, anger and frustration simmering in him.

On the far side of the street he said, "We're not a million miles apart. We're as close as we want to be." But hc could see his words were wasted. He could see it was no use.

They walked in awkward silence for the remainder of the block. He left her at the door of the restaurant. She half-opened the door, then turned and looked at him. "Good-bye, Joseph." Her voice was cool and distant. Final.

He said coldly, "Good-bye." He turned and walked rapidly away.

For a moment Oralee stood looking after him. There was moisture in her eyes. Her mouth was trembling. Resolutely she went into the restaurant, closed the door and crossed to the kitchen.

Her father and mother glanced at her as she came in. Her father, seeing the tears, looked quickly away. Her mother's mouth firmed as she said sharply, "It's getting close to noon. Get the dining room ready. The hotel isn't going to get all the business even if the people are gathered there."

Dutifully, Oralee picked up a tray of silverware and

carried it into the dining room. She began to set each table but her eyes were far away and there were still tears in them.

Joseph glared at each man individually as he passed the Free State Saloon. All of them looked away.

It was over with Oralee, Joseph thought. It was over and he wished it wasn't, but today for the first time he was sure it never could have worked. He'd been deluding himself all along.

He went into the jail. Handy sat with his feet on the desk, his pipe clamped firmly between his teeth. He glanced at Joseph questioningly. "Got it settled?"

Joseph nodded. "It's settled all right. It's finished."

Handy nodded without comment.

Joseph said, "The stage is almost due. Do you think it will get through?"

Handy nodded . "Spotted Horse said we had until tomorrow. He won't attack the stage. All he wants is Holloman and Farley and Weigand."

Joseph went back outside the jail. He stared down the street past Radinski's Hide Yard looking for the lift of dust that would announce the approaching stage.

CHAPTER 15

OLIN MACFARLAND, THE STAGECOACH DRIVER, brought the town of Indian Wells in sight a few minutes before noon. The coach rolled along sedately behind the four horses which he kept at a steady trot. He'd save the gallop for entering the town. There was little enough excitement in towns like Indian Wells. A stagecoach careening behind four galloping horses was a twice weekly diversion he knew all the townspeople looked forward to.

He approached from the south and therefore did not see the Indians north of town until he had almost reached the Indian Creek ford below Radinski's Hide Yard. He stiffened when he finally saw them skylined on a ridge beyond the town, then looked suspiciously up Main Street as though half-expecting an ambush to be awaiting him.

The sight of a crowd of men in front of the Brown Hotel reassured him and his long whip snaked out over the horses' backs. They broke obediently into a gallop, understanding what was expected of them because it was a ritual.

Rocking on its thoroughbraces, the coach rattled noisily up Main Street, with MacFarland yelling and cracking his whip above the backs of the straining teams. Dust lifted behind the coach in a blinding cloud. When MacFarland pulled to a halt in front of the hotel the dust cloud rolled forward, instantly enveloping the coach. MacFarland grinned faintly to himself. He enjoyed these galloping entries into town as much as the townspeople did.

He climbed stiffly down, glancing toward the jail. Pete Handy stood on the walk in front of it, his son Joseph standing at his side. Handy spoke to Joseph, then stepped into the street to cross diagonally toward the hotel.

The coach door opened and the passengers began to alight. MacFarland shouted, "This is Indian Wells. You've got an hour for dinner. You can get it in the hotel or at McDevitt's Restaurant up the street."

Apparently none of the passengers had seen the Indians and MacFarland didn't point them out. The first

passenger out of the coach was Adam Colfax, who
worked for the Kansas City *Courier*. Colfax was
returning from Denver with a feature story he had
written about the western metropolis and its growth.

The second passenger out was Mrs. Charity
Widemeier, middle-aged and heavy, who had buried her
husband, a miner, in the mountains west of Denver and
who was now returning home. Third out was Nate
Goldberg, a salesman for Colt's Patent Fire Arms Mfg.
Co., and last out was Golda Terry, whose profession
was not difficult to guess. She was weary now and her
face was lined and pale. Nevertheless, her glance, from
habit, competently appraised the men nearest her.

Handy reached the coach and MacFarland asked,
"What the hell are all them Indians doin' there?"

"Three buffalo hunters killed an Indian boy. The
Indians want me to turn the hunters over to them."

"What are you goin' to do?"

"I'm not going to turn my prisoners over to any
Indians. I'm holding them for trial."

"What about the coach? You think they'll let it
through?"

"I don't see why not. They've given me until sunup
tomorrow to make up my mind."

MacFarland nodded and began to unhitch the teams.
Fresh horses were already on their way from the stable
with Primitivo Montoya walking behind, driving them.
When they were unhitched, MacFarland drove his two
teams out ahead of the coach, and Montoya backed his
into place. MacFarland helped him hitch them up. By
now the four coach passengers had disappeared.

Pete Handy went into the hotel. The lobby was
jammed with townspeople. Women sat, pale and
frightened, in the leather-covered lobby chairs. Children

106

yelled at their play in the middle of the white-tile lobby floor. The men stood in groups, talking worriedly.

Handy crossed the lobby to the dining room. The four coach passengers had seated themselves at a table and were giving their dinner orders to Mrs. Weisbart. Finished, they got up to head out the back door to the outhouses and washstand. Handy halted them. He said, "You probably know it by now, but if you don't I'll tell you. There are fifty or so Cheyenne north of town. They want three buffalo hunters that are in jail charged with killing an Indian boy. The Cheyenne chief has given me until sunup to make up my mind so I think he'll let the stage go through. But whether you leave on it or not is up to you."

Colfax was a thin, quick-moving man. He said, "What will the Indians do if you refuse?"

Handy shrugged. "If they think their medicine is good enough they might attack the town."

"Then we're taking a chance by staying here?" Handy nodded.

"What if they suspect you of trying to get the buffalo hunters out of town by hiding them on the stage?"

Handy said, "They'll probably think of it. They may stop and search the stage."

The two women's eyes turned scared. The gun salesman said, "What about my samples? If they find my samples . . ."

Handy said, "Leave your samples here. I'll be responsible for them."

The four still seemed undecided so Handy said, "You've got an hour to make up your minds."

He watched them file out. Turning he went back into the lobby and crossed it toward the door. A few people were beginning to drift into the dining room for dinner.

107

Before Handy was halfway across the lobby, Jared Brown intercepted him. "You didn't tell him about the store window and the irons, did you?"

Handy shook his head. "All I told him was that three buffalo hunters had killed an Indian boy and that the Indians wanted them."

Brown released a long sigh of relief. "I hope to God nobody spills the beans."

Handy left him standing there. He went out onto the veranda. Primitivo Montoya was just disappearing into the stable with the wearily plodding teams that had brought the coach to Indian Wells. Olin MacFarland was inspecting the undercarriage of the coach. Handy said, "I gave our passengers a choice. They're going to think about it and let me know."

MacFarland nodded and went back to his work. Handy crossed the street to the jail and went inside.

Adam Colfax was intrigued by the situation Indian Wells. It had all the dramatic possibilities of a damned good story. There were two outhouses behind the hotel.. Mrs. Widemeier went in the women's outhouse first while Golda Terry waited. Nate Goldberg went into the one marked MEN.

Waiting, Colfax realized suddenly that an hour wasn't going to be enough, both to ferret out the story of what was happening in Indian Wells and to eat dinner in the hotel.

Food, then, could wait. He could do without it if necessary. The story wouldn't wait. Goldberg came out and Colfax went in. When he emerged he hurried up the alley instead of going back into the hotel.

He reached Maple Street. Nobody was in sight. Everybody in town was at the hotel, he thought. He'd have to go back and talk to someone at the hotel. He started to turn away. As he did, his eye caught movement on the roof of a small stable on the other side of the street.

It was a boy who looked to be fourteen or fifteen. He was staring north at something Colfax couldn't see, the Indians he supposed. He crossed the street and when he was close enough he asked, "How many do you see?"

The boy turned his head, startled and surprised. He said, "I counted fifty-nine but I think there's more."

"How many men in town?"

"Not much more than that."

"Think the Indians will attack?"

"My pa says they will. 'Less Mr. Handy gives them his prisoners.

"How'd the prisoners happen to kill the Indian?"

"Pa thinks they done it just for fun. They found him out on the prairie alone an' shot him the way a man'll shoot a coyote. He wasn't dead so they brought him back an' put him in the window of the hardware store because they didn't want to turn him loose."

"In the window of the hardware store?" Colfax's voice was incredulous.

"Sure. Didn't you know? They paid my pa to put irons on him an' then they chained him to the floor in the window of the hardware store. When Mr. Handy an' Joseph got back with Luke Kitchen, they seen him there an' took him out. Mr. Handy made Doc come down to the jail an' bandage him but I reckon it was too late by then. The Indian died."

"Didn't anybody in town object? To putting a wounded Indian in a store window like that I mean?"

The boy stared at him. "Why would they object? He was only a Indian."

109

"He was human, boy. He was human just like you. How old did you say he was?"

"Older'n me. A little bit. Maybe a year or two."

"And you think it was all right? Putting him on display like that?"

The boy slid down off the roof. His glance was hostile now. "Why wouldn't it be all right? He was only a damn wild Indian. He'd a killed white people if he'd a got the chance. He just didn't get the chance."

"Where was he wounded? Do you remember?"

"I don't know why I should tell you anything. I don't know you anyway."

Colfax dug in his pocket and found a silver dollar. He held it in his hand, tossing it lightly up and down. "Want this?"

The boy's eyes clung to the dollar greedily. Colfax repeated, "Where was he wounded?"

The boy pointed to his chest, then to his leg. He said, as if trying to earn the dollar quickly, "There was a kind of pink froth comin' from the hole in his chest every time he breathed."

"And the doctor didn't treat him? He didn't do anything?"

"Huh uh. Not until Mr. Handy made him."

"What about the mayor? You have one, don't you? Didn't he do anything?"

"The mayor's Mr. Brown. He owns the hotel. Huh uh. He didn't do anything. Nobody did."

"How long was the Indian there?"

"In the window? Three days, I guess."

Colfax gave the dollar to the boy, who snatched it and quickly ran down the alley toward the back door of the hotel. Colfax stared after him, shocked as he had not been shocked in a long, long time. The inhuman

110

barbarity of what had been done here appalled him. The fact that not one of all the inhabitants in town had objected was more appalling still.

He walked slowly to the corner of Maple and Main. He glanced down the street at the crowd in front of the Brown Hotel and at the crowd across from it in front of the Free State Saloon.

He suddenly realized that the information he had uncovered could be dangerous. People were sure to be ashamed now of what they had done, or rather of what they had failed to do. He backed quickly away from the corner, hoping he had not been seen. He hurried to the alley, intending to return to the back door of the hotel. If the boy didn't talk, everybody would simply assume he had stayed in the outhouse longer than the others had.

He rounded the corner, walking fast. He collided with a squat, muscular, pale-faced man with a neatly trimmed beard. Another man was just behind. This one was burly and muscular and looked like a blacksmith. Colfax tried to hurry past, but the one who looked like a blacksmith grabbed him by the arm. "Wait a minute! Don't be in such a goddam hurry there!"

"I've got to get back to the hotel. The stage is leaving in less than an hour and I've got to eat."

"Plenty of time for that. We'd like to talk to you." Colfax was beginning to feel a little scared. "What about?"

"I understand you been talkin' to my boy."

"Was that your boy? The one on the roof over there watching the Indians?"

"That was him. He says you gave him a dollar. Now why would you do a thing like that?"

"I was just asking him about the Indians."

"Like maybe why were they here?"

111

Colfax nodded mutely.

"And like maybe what they were so worked up about?"

Again Colfax nodded. His throat seemed about to close.

"Did he tell you about the store window an' the chains?"

Colfax was angry at himself. He was angry at the way his hands were shaking, at the way his voice came out, tight and shaking and afraid. But be knew, deep inside of him, that men who will display a mortally wounded Indian as these men had were capable of anything.

The blacksmith said, "You come on down to the hotel with us."

The other man, the one with the beard, asked, "What you going to do with him, Karl?"

"We'll put him in a room upstairs an' lock the door. He'll keep there while we decide what we ought to do."

"You going to tell Brown?"

"Sure. Brown's the one that'll have to decide what's goin' to be done."

Karl and the other man each got hold of one of Colfax's arms. The three walked down the alley to the back door of the hotel. They went in and up a back stairway. Karl and Colfax waited in the upstairs hall while the other man went for a key. When he returned they put him into a room and locked the door.

Adam Colfax was sweating heavily. He could feel his heart thumping inside his chest. He was worse scared than ever before in his life. He wasn't even sure the sheriff would help him. And even if the sheriff would, how was he going to escape from here?

CHAPTER 16

THE STAGECOACH DEPARTED A LITTLE AFTER ONE o'clock. Its exit from town was considerably less spectacular than its arrival had been. Olin MacFarland sat tense and scowling on the box. Inside, the passengers huddled, silent and afraid.

Handy watched the coach depart, unaware that Adam Colfax was not inside. He watched it roll north out of town and saw the small group of braves that pursued it briefly, yelling and firing their guns, before withdrawing to let it proceed. There was no attempt on the Indians' part to halt the coach and search it for three murderers.

He went inside and glanced at Joseph. "They got away all right without getting stopped."

"Did all four of the passengers leave town?"

"I suppose they did. Goldberg left his gun samples here."

"What happens now?"

"I guess the townspeople will keep the pressure on us to turn the prisoners over to the Indians." Handy walked to the window and stared into the street. He still didn't know how the town's dilemma could be resolved. If the Indians didn't get the prisoners they would probably attack the town, but giving up the prisoners would be contrary to everything in which he believed, besides being a violation of his oath. It seemed that no matter what he did, he would be wrong.

His eye caught movement in a second-story side window of the hotel. He saw the window raised, saw a man climb through. The man lowered himself until he was hanging by his bands from the window sill then dropped to the ground. He fell, but he was up almost instantly, limping as he ran through the vacant lot toward the street.

Handy yanked open the door and stepped out onto the walk. He saw faces in the upstairs window from which the man had come and recognized them as those of Spitzer and Grosbeck. The running man was Adam Colfax, who had come in earlier on the stage.

Colfax reached the street and glanced around fearfully. He saw the sheriff and crossed the street toward him, walking now but still limping noticeably.

When he was close enough Handy asked, "What was that all about?"

"Those two men locked me in that room and made me miss the stage. I was afraid to jump at first but I finally decided jumping was less dangerous than staying."

"Did they threaten you?"

"Not directly. They said they were going to talk to Brown, the mayor. They said he would decide what was to be done with me."

"Then I guess you found out about the Indian. Who told you?"

"Spitzer's son."

Handy studied him. Colfax was dusty from his fall and there was anger in his eyes. Handy said, "They don't want the story of that Indian published in the Eastern newspapers."

"Well it's going to be just as soon as I get back to Kansas City with it! I never heard of anything so deliberately barbarous in my life!" Colfax was trembling with indignation now.

Handy frowned at him. Colfax's presence created

114

another problem in addition to those he already had. Colfax was a nervous man, more so now under strain. He was a man unused to this kind of country where physical courage was demanded at some time or other from every man. He was accustomed to the city where everyone was protected by the police.

Handy said, "You'd better stay here, Mr. Colfax. It'll be safer. People feel guilty about that Indian. On top of that, they're scared. I don't think they'd hurt you but there's no use taking the chance."

"What are you going to do about the men who kidnapped me?"

"What do you want me to do?"

"Isn't kidnapping a crime out here?"

"The laws are the same in western Kansas as they are in the eastern part."

"Then arrest those men for kidnapping. If you want me to sign a complaint I will."

Handy nodded. He glanced at Joseph. "Keep him here. Don't let him leave. I don't need any more trouble than I've already got."

Joseph nodded. Adam Colfax frowned.

Handy went out. He crossed swiftly to the hotel and went inside. His glance located Brown and he pushed through the crowd to where the hotelman stood. "Where'd they go?"

"Who?"

"You know who I mean. Grosbeck and Spitzer." Brown gestured toward the rear lobby door with his head and Handy went through the door. Grosbeck and Spitzer were standing in the dark hallway. Both had rifles in their hands.

Handy said, "Come on."

"Come where?"

"Down to the jail. Colfax says you kidnapped him."

"He's a liar."

Handy shook his head. "You'll have to do better than that. I saw him jump from the hotel window. I saw you two looking out right afterward."

Spitzer shifted the rifle in his hands. Handy's voice was sharp. "Don't be stupid, Karl. You've got trouble enough without trying that."

Spitzer's shoulders slumped. Handy said, "Give me the guns."

Both men meekly handed their rifles to him. He said, "All right. Go on down to the jail."

He followed them into the lobby and across it to the door. Once, the men crowded into the lobby tried deliberately to block him from his prisoners but a rough sweep of his arm sent two of them staggering aside. He reached the door half a dozen feet behind Spitzer and Grosbeck.

Out in the street, Spitzer turned his head. "You ain't going to put us in jail, are you?"

"What else do you think I'd do with you?"

"You can't do that! We didn't hurt the little son-of-a-bitch."

"You kidnapped him. He wants to sign a complaint to that effect."

"All we wanted to do was keep him off the stage." Grosbeck chimed in, "So he wouldn't put it in the newspaper about that Indian."

Handy studied the backs of the two men in front of him. "What were you going to do after that? Kill him to shut him up?"

Spitzer said sullenly, "We hadn't got that far. We just wanted him to miss the stage so's we'd have time to figure something out."

116

"And what did you figure out?"

Neither man answered him. They reached the jail and went inside. Handy said, "Joseph, put them in a cell." Joseph went back and unlocked a cell. Spitzer and Grosbeck shuffled into it. Holloman growled, "What the hell's happening?"

"Nothing that concerns you," Handy said. "Step back to the far side of your cell so I can get your trays." Holloman retreated. Handy opened the door and watched the three hunters while Joseph picked up the trays. He relocked the door, then unlocked the door to Kitchen's cell. He picked up Kitchen's tray and afterward relocked his door too.

The front door opened as he returned to the office. Brown came in, followed by Radinski, Doc Bennett, and Lew Gavin, the stableman. Handy stared at the four irritably. "What the hell do you want now?"

Brown scowled, looked at the others, then glanced back at Handy again. He said, "First of all, we want you to get those Indians to leave. Give the three buffalo hunters to them. It's better than having them attack the town."

Handy waited. Brown said, "Next, turn Grosbeck and Spitzer loose. They didn't kidnap that newspaperman. All they did was lock him up for a little while."

Handy said, "And?"

"Give the newspaperman to us."

Handy asked, "And what will you do with him?"

"That isn't your concern."

"Kill him?" Handy fished in his pocket for his pipe. "Who's going to do the killing? You, Mr. Brown? Or will you get Spitzer to do your dirty work like the hunters did?"

"Nobody said anything about killing."

117

"But you want him shut up, don't you? How do you plan to accomplish that without killing him?"

All four men looked intensely uneasy. Not one of them would meet Handy's eyes. Handy glanced at Colfax. "Want to go with them, Mr. Colfax?"

"Are you out of your mind? They're planning to murder me."

"I don't know how you can believe that of them. These are respectable men. One's a doctor. Another is the mayor. A third runs the hide yard and the fourth is the stableman. They wouldn't murder anyone, Mr. Colfax."

Colfax stared at him suspiciously.

Handy scowled angrily at the four townsmen. "I don't know what you've got in mind. I can't believe you'd really kill this man. But the answer to all three of your demands is no. And I'd suggest you start making plans to fight off those Indians."

Brown said sullenly, "We were only going to try and buy him off."

Handy said, "Get out of here."

The four shuffled sullenly out the door. Handy kicked it shut.

Colfax was thoroughly frightened. He said, "I want to get out of this town. I want to get out now."

"I'm afraid that isn't possible. You'd never make it alone and I can't go with you myself."

"What about your son?"

"I need him here."

Colfax walked nervously to the window and stared outside. He spoke without turning. "Would they really kill me, Mr. Handy?"

"Hell, I don't know what they'd do. They're scared. They're ashamed of what they allowed to happen to that

118

Indian. But I've quit trying to predict what people are going to do. Brown fought in the war and so did Gavin. Bennett was a surgeon. All three have seen their share of killing, so I wouldn't say they were incapable of killing you. But they probably did intend to try and buy you off." He gestured with his head toward the cells out back. "Those two, Grosbeck and Spitzer, are something else. And maybe that's why Brown wanted me to turn them loose. Maybe he figured they'd do his dirty work."

"What happens now?"

"We wait. We've got until sunup tomorrow."

"What good will waiting do?"

"It'll give the townspeople time to prepare a defense."

"Do you really intend to hold out? You intend to let the Indians attack the town?"

Handy studied him. "What would *you* do, Mr. Colfax?"

Colfax started to speak, then closed his mouth. A flush crept up into his face. Handy asked, "What were you going to say?"

"I was going to say you should turn the three buffalo hunters over to the Indians. But that wouldn't be any more moral than turning me over to Brown and his friends." He was silent a moment.

Handy said, "Make yourself comfortable, Mr. Colfax. But don't leave the jail." He glanced at Joseph, sitting relaxed and comfortable in the swivel chair. "I'll take the trays back to the restaurant. Then I'm going to make a circle around the town."

Joseph nodded without getting up. He looked relaxed but Handy knew every muscle and nerve in his body was tight as a fiddlestring.

119

CHAPTER 17

HANDY RETURNED THE TRAYS TO MCDEVITT'S Restaurant. Oralee was waiting on customers. She avoided looking at him. He put the trays down on a table and went back outside. In one way he was sorry Joseph had broken up with Oralee but in another he was relieved. He knew it never could have worked.

He headed north up Main, walking in the middle of the street. Fifteen or twenty young Indians were galloping back and forth along the ridge, showing off. Handy stopped at Box Elder Street. It marked the northern edge of town and was overgrown with weeds. He pulled out his pipe and packed it deliberately. He lighted it and puffed for a moment, his eyes squinted against the smoke.

Suddenly he stiffened. His eyes narrowed as he stared at the ridgetop where the young Indians were. A single figure was riding through them toward the town.

Even at this distance, there was something familiar, something recognizable about that solitary rider. It could be none other than Bird Woman. Swiftly Handy began to walk through the high grass and weeds toward her.

She kept her horse at a walk, ignoring the young Indians galloping a circle around her, ignoring their taunts and shouts. She left them behind and came down the slope, meeting Handy a couple of hundred yards from town.

Her eyes clung to his and there were tears in them, silent tears that spilled over and ran across her cheeks. He realized that she had feared she might not see him again alive. She slid from the back of her horse and into his arms. She was warm, and trembling, and he knew she had longed for him all these months as desperately as he had longed for her. He tilted her face up toward him and asked, "Why did you come?"

"I was afraid for you and for our son."

Her presence created another problem and although he already had problems enough, he was glad that she had come. He took her horse's reins with one hand, her arm with the other and headed back toward town. She asked, "What is happening?"

"They want the buffalo hunters that killed Fat Bear. They say if they do not get them they will attack the town."

"Is Joseph all right?"

"He's fine. He's down at the jail."

"You do not mind that I have come?"

He said, "I'm glad you came. I have missed you."

"I will try to stay out of the way." She was looking toward the small three-room house he and Joseph shared. The house stood on the corner of Main and Elm, just a block from the edge of town.

Handy shook his head. "Huh uh. I don't want you staying there. If the Indians attack I want you someplace where you'll be safe."

Her eyes questioned him. He said, "You can stay at the hotel tonight. By tomorrow this will probably be all over with."

He found himself wishing that he could leave with her right now, that he could put Indian Wells behind him forever and go back to the village of Half Yellow Face with her to stay.

But that was only a dream, a dream that would not come true. They passed McDevitt's Restaurant and the

121

Kansas Mercantile and Handy crossed the street diagonally with her toward the Brown Hotel.

He felt like a stranger as he pushed through the crowd on the hotel veranda and followed Bird Woman into the lobby. Her clothes seemed wild and strange here in this crowded place and he felt like an alien among these people who looked at him and at his wife with such hostility. Anger flared in him, anger that he resolutely controlled.

They crossed to the desk. Davey Locke looked up. Handy said, "I want a room for my wife."

Davey looked scared. He stared at Bird Woman and then at Handy. He swallowed, and forced a smile. Handy said, "You heard me, didn't you?"

"I . . . I got to see Mr. Brown." Davey fled, ducking from behind the desk and crossing the lobby at a shambling run. Brown was on the far side of the lobby. Davey talked to him excitedly a moment. Then the two approached the desk.

Handy's anger was growing and becoming more difficult to control. Brown came around behind the desk and Handy said evenly, "I want a room for my wife."

Brown's face flushed and he swallowed the way Davey had earlier. He said, "Pete, I can't . . . she's an Indian and you know how these folks feel about Indians."

Bird Woman's hand pulled gently at Handy's sleeve. He glanced at her and saw the painful embarrassment in her face. He said softly, "God damn you, Brown, give me a key before I come around there and mop up the floor with you."

Brown started to speak but Handy reached across the desk and grabbed him by the shirtfront. Brown said hastily, "All right! All right! But don't blame me if . . ."

122

He stopped. Handy released him and he took a key from one of the cubbyholes. He gave it to the sheriff with a shaking hand.

Handy led Bird Woman across the crowded lobby toward the stairs. His angry eyes dared anyone to say anything or interfere. Nobody did. He followed her up the stairs to the room which was number 8. He unlocked the door and they went in. He closed the door behind him.

She stood for a moment in the middle of the room, her back to him. He waited, and after a moment she turned. She looked at him, then ran into his arms.

He held her tightly for a long, long time, wanting her and knowing she wanted him but knowing too that this was not the time. At last he released her, walked to the window and stared down into the street. His hands, usually so steady, were trembling.

The street was virtually deserted. No children played in it. No women crossed it, going from store to store. Handy said, "I've got to get back down to the jail. I'll see you at suppertime."

She smiled, but her eyes were worried and the smile was forced. He kissed her, thinking that he had been a fool. He would be a fool no more. If he was still alive when this was over with, he would go back with her to the village of Half Yellow Face.

He went quickly out the door and down the stairs. He jostled several townspeople between the foot of the stairway and the door. He was so angry he didn't even hear their muttering.

But as he stalked across the street toward the jail, he admitted reluctantly that he was putting too much blame on the people of the town. It was true that they had not protested the cruelty of putting the wounded Indian in the store window. It was true that they had made Joseph feel alien. It was also true that they had suffered much at the hands of the Indians and that hatred does not quickly die.

Joseph had tried to right the wrong that had been done Fat Bear by taking his body home for burial and he had permitted it. But all they had managed to do was to make things worse. More violence would result. And afterward reprisals would be taken against the Indians by the military at Fort Hays.

It was a circle that had no end. You always came back to your starting point.

It was now midafternoon. The street, in spite of the time of year, was hot and the air was still. Handy went into the jail. Colfax was asleep on the office couch. Handy pushed his hat back on his head and mopped his sweating brow with the back of his hand. Joseph said softly, "That was Mother, wasn't it?"

"Uh huh."

"Did they give you any trouble at the hotel?"

Handy started to deny it, then stopped. He said, "Brown tried to refuse her a room. He changed his mind."

Joseph grinned faintly, knowing what had made Brown change his mind. Handy sat down in the swivel chair that Joseph had just vacated and put his booted feet up on the desk. Joseph crossed to the door and stepped outside. He stared north up the street. There was a line of mounted Indians silhouetted against the sky. It stretched out for almost a quarter mile. He made a rapid count. There were a hundred and thirty-three Indians in the line. He went back into the jail, not missing the way the silent crowd in front of the hotel was staring north at the Indians. He said softly, "They just put on a show of

124

force. I counted a hundred and thirty-three of them."

Handy nodded wearily. "There'll be a couple of hundred by dawn tomorrow."

"Can the town fight off that many Indians?"

Handy nodded. "The town can fight them off but there are going to be a lot of casualties on both sides. And there are bound to be some buildings burned."

Joseph began to pace nervously back and forth. Handy said, "You're giving me the willies. Go on up and see your ma. She's in room 8."

Joseph nodded. He went out into the street and headed across toward the hotel. Handy remained in the swivel chair.

Out back in his cell, Holloman yelled, "Hey, Sheriff!"

"What?"

"What's going on out there?"

"More Indians."

"How many now?"

"Joseph counted a hundred and thirty-three."

"Jesus! That's more than there are people in town." Handy didn't reply. There was a silence and then Holloman asked, "You thinkin' about givin' us to them?"

"I'm not, but I think I should. You three aren't worth getting good men killed. Or buildings burned."

"You think they'll attack the town?"

"They'll attack. At sunup tomorrow."

"How about lettin' us out? You could use our guns."

"How long do you think you'd last out there? The townspeople want to give you to the Indians."

"We can take care of ourselves."

"You're not going to get the chance. You're going to stay right where you are." After that he could hear Holloman and the other two talking softly among

125

themselves, but he couldn't make out what they said. Colfax awoke but he didn't get up off the couch.

Handy closed his eyes. Memories paraded through his thoughts. He remembered how it had been when he first went to live with the Cheyenne. He remembered the way Bird Woman had been when she was a girl. He remembered her, big bellied with Joseph, and he remembered the night Joseph had been born. A small smile touched his mouth.

He dozed, then slept, and when he awoke the late afternoon sun was streaming into the jail. He was stiff from sitting in the chair.

He got up, and stretched, and got himself a drink of water out of the bucket on the washstand. He hung the dipper up, stretched again and went to the door. He could hear someone snoring in one of the cells out back. Colfax had gone back to sleep.

He wondered where Joseph was. He had been gone almost two hours. Handy supposed he and his mother had found lots of things to talk about.

The sun was hot. Noise poured from the open doors of the Free State Saloon. There was a crowd on the veranda of the Brown Hotel, resting in the shade.

A little twinge of uneasiness touched Handy's mind. It wasn't like Joseph to stay away so long. He considered going to the hotel to look for him, then discarded the idea. Joseph was all right. He was letting the tension get to him.

He went back into the jail. He got himself another drink of water, then sat down and packed his pipe. He looked at his watch. It was almost five o'clock. Colfax sat up and rubbed his eyes. "What time is it?"

"Five." Handy frowned, wondering about Joseph again. It was getting close to suppertime. Joseph would

126

have to be going after meals for the prisoners.

Once more he thought about going to look for Joseph and once more he put the thought aside. He didn't dare leave the jail unguarded now. Too many men in town favored turning the buffalo hunters over to the Indians. Too many wanted Spitzer and Grosbeck released. Too many wanted to shut Colfax up.

He glanced up as the door opened. He put his feet down on the floor. Brown came in, accompanied by Radinski, Bennett, and Gavin. Several others had to remain outside in the street. Brown said, "We want you to turn those hunters over to the Indians, Pete. We want you to do it now."

Handy shook his head.

"Then we want you to resign."

Again Handy shook his head.

Brown said, "Pete, you're tough. But don't get the idea that we're not as tough as you. We can force you out."

Handy got to his feet. "You try that, Brown. You try."

"We've got our backs to the wall, Pete. Our lives are at stake and so is our property. We're not going to lose everything for three murdering buffalo hunters. We're not going to let that newspaperman go back East and ruin us."

Handy waited. At last he said, "Get to it, Brown. Say what you came to say."

"We've got Joseph, Pete. We've got him locked up in a room at the hotel. And we've got your wife. Either you turn those hunters and the newspaperman over to us, or . . . well, I can't answer for what might happen to Joseph and your wife."

Handy realized that he had half-expected this. Even so, he could feel the cold fury growing in his mind. He

127

fought it down.

He glanced at Colfax, sitting on the edge of the office couch. The man was scared. He licked his lips, looked at Brown, then back at Handy again.

Handy suddenly knew how the townspeople planned to get rid of the newspaperman. They meant to turn him over to the Indians along with Holloman, Farley, and Weigand. That would eliminate him and they wouldn't have to murder him.

He said, "All of you, get out of here. Get out, before . . .!"

The four began to back uneasily out of the jail. Brown said, "Don't be foolish, Pete. Don't risk . . ."

"Get out!"

"You've got until midnight to make up your mind. That's all, Pete. Midnight."

Handy got suddenly to his feet. Brown turned and plunged through the door into the street. Handy cursed sourly. He'd thought things couldn't get much worse but he'd been wrong.

CHAPTER 18

JOSEPH DIDN'T GET AS FAR AS HIS MOTHER'S ROOM. HE reached the stairway, pushing through the crowd, and suddenly felt a gun muzzle thrust into his back. Sol Radinski's accented voice said, "It's a gun, Joseph. Don't do anything foolish and everything will be all right."

A hand withdrew his gun from its holster. Brown's voice said, "All right, Joseph. Go on upstairs to your mother's room."

Joseph turned his head. "What's this all about?"

"We need hostages to make your father turn the buffalo hunters over to the Indians. You and your mother are the hostages."

The gun muzzle dug deeper into his back. Resignedly, Joseph climbed the stairs, followed closely by Radinski and Brown. He stopped at the door of room 8. Brown said, "Knock, Joseph. And don't do anything stupid. We don't want to hurt anyone."

Joseph said, "Keep her out of it. You can keep me as a hostage, but leave her out of it."

Brown shook his head. Joseph looked from Brown to Radinski. Both men's faces were frightened, but both were stubborn too. He knocked and when the door opened, stepped inside. Brown removed the key from the lock and pulled the door shut. Joseph heard the key turn in the lock.

Bird Woman looked questioningly at him. Joseph said, "We're hostages. They want Pa to turn the three hunters over to the Indians."

Her eyes were worried now. Joseph said, "They won't hurt us. Not unless they're out of their minds. They know what he'd do to anyone that hurt either one of us." He said the words to reassure her but he knew they weren't true. Brown and Radinski had to be desperate to risk taking the sheriff's wife and son as hostages. And desperate men might do anything.

He walked to the window and stared down into the street. It was late afternoon and the room was hot. Except for a few in front of the hotel, except for half a dozen men standing in front of the saloon, the street was deserted.

He'd made a mistake in taking Fat Bear home for burial. By doing so, he had precipitated a situation that could only result in bloodshed and destruction. Innocent people were going to die in Indian Wells. Indians would also die in the attack tomorrow. The town might be destroyed. And even if the Indians won, they'd lose. Soldiers would march on their villages. Ten Indians would die for every white person they had killed.

The feeling that he was responsible for it was a weight in Joseph's thoughts. Whatever happened would be his fault. Those who died would die because of him. Somehow he had to stop it from happening. But how? Particularly now that he was locked up here. He couldn't drop from the window the way Colfax had because his window faced the street. If he dropped from it he'd land right in the middle of the crowd.

He turned away from the window. He crossed to the door and tried the knob. He got down on one knee and looked through the keyhole. He could see nothing and suddenly realized that Brown and Radinski had left the key in the lock.

There was an old newspaper on the dresser top. He got it and slid a sheet of it under the door. Then, with his pocket knife, he poked at the key until it dropped. Carefully he pulled the newspaper back into the room. The key was lying on it. He picked it up and unlocked the door. He opened it and peered out into the hall.

The hall was deserted, but he could hear the murmur of voices in the lobby. He motioned for his mother to remain where she was, then went out into the hall. He eased along it until he could see the lobby stairs.

He could also see part of the lobby crowd, women with drawn faces and frightened eyes, children turned quiet by their elders' fears. Some of the townspeople were trying to talk to each other in order to calm themselves. Some just sat staring into space, twisting a handkerchief or gripping their hands together. Nobody

130

seemed to know what to do. They all undoubtedly hoped that somehow a showdown with the Indians could be prevented by forcing the sheriff to turn over his prisoners to them.

Joseph retreated to the room. He put the key back in the lock and closed the door. Frowning, he tried to decide what he should do. He could get away, he supposed, if he tried. There was a chance that he'd be caught but if he was willing to take the risk, he could probably get away.

Getting his mother away was something else. Right now he didn't feel justified in taking the chance that she'd be hurt. The door was unlocked, though, and maybe later a chance would come.

He walked to the window again and stared across at the jail. He couldn't see how his father was going to get out of this dilemma. There were only two impossible alternatives.

Adam Colfax was scared, but he was discovering that living in a state of sustained terror is all but impossible. He had never come up against the threat of raw violence before. But today he had faced that threat and had managed to function in spite of it. He had slipped away from the hotel and had found out what the town was trying to hide from him. He had been caught and imprisoned in a room at the hotel, but he had escaped. He might be ashamed of his fear but, he told himself stoutly, he needn't be ashamed of the way he had performed.

He had even been able to get a little sleep. He smiled ruefully to himself. He needn't take credit for that, he thought. Traveling by stagecoach was an exhausting ordeal. After three days in a rocking, careening stagecoach, a man could sleep whenever he closed his eyes.

He studied Pete Handy's face, remembering Brown's demand that he be turned over to them along with the buffalo hunters who had killed the young Indian. He asked, "What are you going to do?"

Handy turned his shaggy head. He said, "Hell, I don't know. I'm damned if I do and I'm damned if I don't." His eyes studied Colfax briefly. "What would you do if you was me?"

Colfax hadn't thought of the problem in those terms. He did so now. Handy was watching him. Colfax said, "I hope I'd do what I thought was right."

"What's right? Letting those Indians attack the town?"

"Turning the hunters over to the Indians to be tortured and killed isn't right either."

"And you along with them. Isn't that what you meant to say?"

"Maybe. What's wrong with that? I haven't committed any crime. They just want me dead so I can't expose them in the newspapers. But it's hard to believe that respectable men like that would kill me in cold blood."

"They wouldn't. They'd turn you over to the Indians along with Holloman and Farley and Weigand. The Indians would get rid of you for them. They wouldn't have to dirty their hands with it."

"You don't think much of them, do you?"

Handy shook his head.

Colfax walked to the window and stared into the street. Handy said, "I've got to go up to the restaurant and get meals for the prisoners. Do you want to stay here or go with me? I could use your help carrying the

132

trays."

Colfax didn't hesitate. "I'll go with you."

Handy went out, followed by the newspaperman. He turned and locked the door. He didn't like leaving the jail unguarded but the prisoners had to eat.

The sun had dropped behind the western plain. The sky flamed orange as the sun's last rays stained the clouds. Handy walked up the street toward McDevitt's Restaurant. Colfax kept pace with him, staring uneasily at the crowd in front of the hotel and at the crowd in front of the Free State Saloon.

Men gave way for them in front of the saloon. They passed through. Handy heard some grumbling, but could make out no words.

There were half a dozen men in the restaurant, all buffalo hunters. They probably didn't want to eat down at the hotel with the townspeople, Handy thought. Oralee was not visible so he stuck his head into the kitchen. He said, "Meals for the prisoners, and for Colfax and myself. Eight in all. Coffee while we're waiting." He made it a point not to say please. He was damned, tonight, if he was going to say please to anyone.

He sat down at a nearby table with Colfax. He could feel the buffalo hunters watching him. Like the townspeople, they were wondering what he was going to do. The only difference was, they wanted him to refuse to turn the hunters over to the Indians. The townspeople wanted him to give them up.

He wished he knew, himself, what he was going to do. He knew what was right. That was the easy part. But if he did what was right a lot of people were going to die. And he couldn't see anything right in that.

Oralee brought two cups of coffee and put them down

133

in front of Handy and the newspaperman. Handy looked up at her. She flushed painfully, looked away, then determinedly looked back at him. She licked her lips and finally said haltingly, "I'm sorry, Mr. Handy. About Joseph and me, I mean. Mama and Papa said . . . They said I wasn't to see him any more."

Handy said sympathetically, "It's all right, Oralee. It wouldn't have worked anyway."

"Maybe . . . maybe if I was different . . ."

Handy said, "We're all what we are, Oralee. We can't change. Don't feel too badly about it."

Tears filled Oralee's eyes. Her chin quivered. She started to say something, choked on it and turned. She ran into the kitchen without looking back.

Colfax asked, "What was that all about?"

"She and Joseph were going together."

Colfax said, "You were right. It never would have worked. I can't imagine a more unlikely couple than your son Joseph and that girl."

Handy sipped the scalding coffee. He couldn't get the choice he had to make out of his thoughts. Colfax said, "Joseph needs an Indian girl."

Handy nodded. "I guess I made a mistake when I tried to raise Joseph among the whites."

"It might have worked back East. But not out here. There's too much bitter feeling against the Indians."

"Maybe when this is over with . . ." Handy's voice trailed off. It was too late. Besides, he couldn't bear to leave Bird Woman, and he doubted if Joseph would go back East alone.

He finished his coffee and sat staring blankly into space. Colfax watched him worriedly, knowing his own fate hung on the decision Handy made.

At last, Oralee began carrying trays in from the

kitchen. She brought two at a time, stacking them up four to a stack. Handy picked up four and Colfax picked up the other four. Oralee held the door for them.

Handy hoped ruefully that he didn't have to arrest anybody else. Carrying eight trays three times a day was work enough.

CHAPTER 19

HANDY FED THE PRISONERS AND WHILE THEY WERE eating gulped his own supper hungrily. Colfax seemed to have little appetite. He picked listlessly at his food and finally gave up.

Handy gathered up the trays from the prisoners' cells one by one and stacked them on his desk. By the time he had finished, it was dark outside.

He looked at Colfax. "Mind helping me carry them back to the restaurant?"

Colfax shook his head. He picked up four of the trays and carried them out the door, which Handy held for him. Handy carried the other four trays outside, put them down on the walk, then carefully locked the door.

There was no longer a crowd in front of the hotel. Nor was anyone on the walk outside the saloon. But inside it was packed with loud-talking men. Buffalo hunters were grouped clannishly at one end of the room, townsmen at the other.

Handy had no fear for the safety of either Joseph or his wife. The townspeople weren't going to hurt them yet. But he did dislike the thought of having it said later that his decision had been influenced by the threat against their lives.

He was under no illusions as to what would happen

when this was all over with. If he had given the buffalo hunters to the Indians he would be accused of sacrificing them cold-bloodedly when there was no need for it. If he had refused to surrender them and the town had been attacked, he would be accused of causing the trouble by permitting Joseph to take the dead Indian home for burial and by refusing to turn the killers over to the Indians. Either way, he would be in the wrong.

The two reached McDevitt's Restaurant, carried the trays inside and put them on a table near the door. They went back out, without being spoken to by anyone.

Handy paused long enough to fish his pipe from his pocket and pack it carefully. Colfax found a cigar, bit off the end and lighted it. He waited apprehensively.

Handy said, "I'm going to the hotel and get Joseph and my wife."

"Isn't that taking an awful chance? The townspeople might . . ."

Handy said, "They won't do anything. They're not ready yet."

"Then why take a chance of stirring something up? If your wife and son are in no danger from the townspeople?"

"I said they weren't in any danger now."

Colfax's voice came out scared. "Do you want me to help?"

Handy nodded. "I want you to go in the front door of the hotel. I want you to get their attenion. That way I can surprise them and there'll be less chance that some hothead will take it up."

Colfax's knees were shaking. He hoped Handy didn't see. He said, "All right."

"Give me ten minutes to get set at the back door of the hotel. Got a watch?"

Colfax pulled an ornate gold watch from his vest pocket. He opened the hunting case and held the watch so that the small amount of light coming from the restaurant windows illuminated its face. He said, "Ten minutes," and hoped his voice didn't sound as shaky as he felt.

Handy crossed the street, disappearing almost immediately into the darkness. Colfax stepped back into the shadows beside the restaurant wall. He waited for what seemed an eternity, then stepped forward and looked at his watch again. Less than five minutes had elapsed.

He wished he'd had the sense to keep his damn mouth shut. He didn't want to go into the hotel all alone. He knew the townspeople wanted him. He knew they intended to turn him over to the Indians along with the buffalo hunters that the sheriff had in jail.

He waited in the shadows for what seemed another eternity, then looked at his watch again. Only a minute of the ten remained. He waited, counting off the seconds in his mind. When the minute was up, he crossed the street toward the open door of the Brown Hotel.

He climbed the steps to the veranda, wanting to turn and run, angrily controlling his fear. He crossed the veranda and stepped into the lobby.

It was a minute or so before anybody noticed him. He could hear a woman weeping, and several children whimpering. Worst of all was the look he saw on the faces of the people gathered here. It was a look he couldn't fail to recognize, one of terror and uncertainty.

Silence began among those nearest him and spread like the ripples in a pond until the whole lobby was as silent as a tomb. A voice shouted, "There he is! Grab the son-of-abitch before he gets away again!"

Several men started toward him. Colfax looked frantically toward the rear lobby door. Handy appeared in it suddenly to his vast relief. The sheriff roared, "Hold it! Hold it right where you are!"

The men who had started toward Colfax stopped. They turned their heads.

Handy said, "Get the key at the desk, Mr. Colfax, and go up and let Joseph and my wife out of whatever room they're in."

Colfax crossed the lobby to the desk. A man behind it handed him a key. A number 8 was stamped on the tag attached.

He went up the stairs and along the hall until he came to room 8. A key was already in the lock. He tried to unlock the door and failed. He tried the knob and the door opened. Surprised, Colfax looked in and saw the sheriff's son and an Indian woman standing in the middle of the room. He said, "I'm Adam Colfax. The sheriff sent me up to unlock your door and let you out."

"Is he downstairs?"

Colfax nodded. "Holding a gun on the crowd."

Joseph said, "Come on, Ma," and led her out into the hall. Colfax followed them down the stairs.

Handy still stood at the rear of the lobby just inside the door. He said, "Thanks, Mr. Colfax. Now, just go down to the jail with Joseph and my wife. I'll be along right away."

Colfax stared at him a moment. Then he turned and followed Joseph and the Indian woman across the lobby and out into the street.

Handy remained still for several minutes after the three had left. He had a gun in his hand but he didn't know whether he could have used it. Here in this crowded lobby, a stray shot could hit anyone, a woman or a child.

There was anger in some of the people facing him. In others there was bitterness. Others looked at him beseechingly. And suddenly he knew that however terrible it would be for him to give up three of his prisoners, it was something he was going to have to do. The commandant at Fort Hays had refused to help. The Indians were right outside the town. To refuse the Indians his prisoners would be to ensure a dawn attack.

He would have to give up the prisoners, he thought, but he would not give up the newspaperman. He would compromise his oath enough to save the town's life but he would not compromise it to save the town's reputation.

Joseph and Bird Woman and Colfax must have reached the jail by now. He shoved his gun into its holster and walked wearily across the lobby to the door. He had made up his mind what he was going to do but he couldn't bring himself to tell these people yet. He still clung to the forlorn hope that help would come from Fort Hays, that the Indians would withdraw, that something would happen to make unnecessary the surrender of his prisoners.

Yet he knew, deep inside himself, that nothing was going to happen. No help was coming from Fort Hays. The Indians weren't going to withdraw.

He walked slowly toward the jail through the early darkness. Somewhere a cricket chirped. A dog barked several blocks away.

He had been a lawman a good part of his life but after tomorrow, he thought, he could never be a lawman again. He would be known from one end of the frontier to the other as the man who had surrendered three white prisoners to the Indians, to be brutally tortured and killed. Forgotten would be the crime the three had committed against a helpless Indian boy. Forgotten would be the fact that the surrender had saved the town of Indian Wells.

He halted in the middle of the street directly in front of the jail, delaying what he knew he had to do, staring north beyond the edge of town. The Cheyenne had several fires going on the ridge. In the flickering yellow firelight he could see the moving figures of the Indians. He wondered how many were out there now.

Reluctantly, he walked toward the jail. He took a moment to light his dead pipe before opening the door. Then he stepped inside.

He sensed, rather than saw, the figure immediately beside the door as he opened it. He started to turn . . . A blow struck his head, stunning him, driving him to his knees. His hand went to his gun but there was no longer any strength in him. He couldn't make his eyes focus properly. He couldn't force his hand to draw the gun. He couldn't even turn his head to see who had struck him down.

He tried to get up and staggered forward, stunned and helpless physically. But he still could hear and he still could think and he heard Joseph say, "I'm sorry, Pa. I'm sorry I had to hit you like that. But it's the only way."

He collapsed, falling forward on his face. He felt Bird Woman's presence beside him. He heard a cell door being unlocked. He heard Joseph's harsh voice ordering the prisoners out of the cell, one by one. Colfax must be helping Joseph, he thought dazedly. He fought to regain his fading consciousness, wanting to tell Joseph that one man couldn't possibly force three reluctant prisoners to leave the jail and walk out onto the prairie to be turned over to the Indians. He wanted to tell Joseph that he had decided the only way to save the town was to turn the prisoners over to the Indians, that he would help. But no words came out. He could only groan.

He heard the metallic sounds of handcuffs and chains. He vaguely saw a man stagger across the office in the direction of the door, propelled from behind by some powerful force. A second man staggered after the first and then a third.

Joseph was yelling at them now. The door opened and the three prisoners burst out into the street.

Handy managed to say thickly, "Help me! Help me up!"

Bird Woman put her arm around him and, struggling, helped him to his feet. Staggering, the two went toward the open door.

Handy banged violently against the doorjamb and hung there, fighting desperately to regain full consciousness. In the street, Joseph had untied and mounted his horse. He rode the first of the prisoners down and tied his manacles to the end of his lariat that he held coiled up in his hand. Dragging him, he rode the others down. Each time it was a scuffle and a fight. Each time Joseph's fist subdued a struggling hunter long enough to tie him to the end of the rope.

The whole disorderly process seemed to take a long time. In reality it took less than five minutes in all. At the end of it, Handy was strong enough to shout, "Joseph! Wait!"

Joseph heeled his horse up the middle of the street, dragging the three cursing, struggling hunters behind. One fell down and skidded along until the others helped him to his feet. Joseph called back, "It's my doing, Pa. It's up to me to make it right."

Handy cursed his helplessness. He staggered toward

his horse, fidgeting nervously at the tie rail in front of
the jail. Bird Woman pleaded with him to wait, but he
shook her hands away. He grabbed the saddlehorn and
hung on. Waves of weakness washed over him. He
couldn't make it yet. He couldn't make it but he had to
try. Thickly he said, "Untie the reins. Goddamit, untie
the reins!"

She untied them and handed them to him. He put a
foot into the stirrup, still clinging to the saddlehorn. He
clenched his teeth and forced himself to mount.

The horse turned and started up the street. The town
and its dim lights tilted before Handy's eyes. He was
falling, and knew it but he couldn't stop himself. He hit
the dust of the street and tasted grit between his teeth
before everything went black.

CHAPTER 20

JOSEPH RODE WITH THE END OF THE ROPE DALLIED
hard around his saddlehorn. He kept it tight, forcing the
buffalo hunters to move at a shuffling run. If they got
any slack they might succeed in untying the rope from
their manacles.

Despite being out of breath, Holloman managed to
yell frantically as they neared the upper limits of the
town, "Deputy, for God's sake, don't turn us over to
them savages! Deputy!"

Joseph didn't answer him. He was hoping he hadn't
hit his father too hard. He knew that a blow on the head
could cause permanent injury or even death. But he also
was aware that he couldn't have taken prisoners from
Pete Handy while he was conscious. Threatening him
with a gun would have done no good at all.

He consoled himself with the memory of his father's shouted demand for him to wait. Handy must not have been too badly hurt or he couldn't have regained consciousness so rapidly. Yet the very fact that he had regained consciousness put an added urgency into getting the prisoners to the Indians. If Pete Handy was conscious he wouldn't waste any time coming after Joseph and his prisoners.

All three of the hunters were yelling at him now, yelling incoherently. They were too out of breath to make any sense but Joseph knew what they were trying to say. They were begging him not to turn them over to the Indians. They were thoroughly terrified. Their bravado had completely disappeared.

The town was now a quarter mile behind. Still Joseph heard no pursuing hoofbeats. He saw nothing of his father coming on behind.

What would he do if Pete Handy came, he asked himself. Would he try to overcome his father a second time? He shook his head. No. He couldn't fight his father over these three prisoners. He'd have to give them up. He'd have to let his father decide what was to be done with them.

He could see the fires on the ridge more plainly now and he could more plainly hear the yells of the Indians. Some of them were dancing tentatively around the fires, working up to a big war dance later on tonight. He wasn't a bit too soon in getting the three prisoners to them, he thought. If they danced all night they'd be too worked up to ride peacefully away from Indian Wells tomorrow. They'd attack the town anyway, just for the hell of it.

In desperation, all three of the prisoners laid down and forced him to drag them along the ground. The rope stretched taut and creaked with the strain on it. The horse leaned forward, pulling like a work animal. But he did not stop.

This way, Joseph traveled a couple of hundred yards. He was now less than half a mile from the nearest of the fires on the ridge. The horse slowed but Joseph dug spurs into his sides and forced him to go on.

One by one the hunters struggled to their feet. Once more they shuffled along behind the horse, trying to cry out, too out of breath to make much sense. Joseph couldn't help his feeling satisfaction that they were so thoroughly terrified. They must be experiencing, he thought, the same terror that young Indian had felt when they manacled him and put him into the window of the hardware store.

Yet at the same time, he was ashamed of what he was about to do to them. He thought he knew what the manner of their death would be. The young Cheyenne weren't going to be satisfied with simply and quickly killing them. Fat Bear's friends were among the Indians on the ridge. Members of his family were also there. The deaths of the hunters would not be easy nor would they be quick.

Now only a quarter mile remained. Joseph urged his horse forward at a slightly faster pace. If he did not get this over soon he might change his mind.

His own life among the whites was finished now, but he felt no sadness because of that. He felt, instead, a vast relief. He'd never really wanted to live among the whites. He had always preferred the Indian way. He had only lived with the whites to please his father, because Handy wanted it that way.

He'd go with Bird Woman and live once more in the village of Half Yellow Face. Pete Handy could stay on as sheriff in Indian Wells. There would be no reason he could not. He'd get credit for having saved the town without bearing the stigma of having surrendered his prisoners to the Indians. His life would not, at least, be ruined by the things that had happened in the last few days.

Joseph grinned ruefully to himself. Everything sounded fine the way he'd worked it out in his mind, but he knew it wouldn't turn out that way. It was too easy and too pat.

Suddenly, from ahead, a shrill cry arose. It came first from a single throat but it was taken up almost immediately by half a hundred other throats. They sounded like a pack of coyotes on a ridge, he thought, only there were never this many coyotes howling and barking all at once.

He drew his horse to a halt. He was still fifty yards away but he could see the painted faces of the Indians in the firelight. He could see in them a fierce excitement over the prospect of attacking the town tomorrow.

And he realized something he had not realized before. They were not threatening the town solely because of what had happened to Fat Bear. Behind their eagerness to attack Indian Wells was a half century of broken promises and abuse. The whites had killed the buffalo and stolen the Indians' land. They had reduced a once proud people to a race of beggars, dependent for life upon the doubtful bounty of the white man's government.

Halted, Joseph shouted in the Cheyenne tongue, "I have brought to you the hunters who killed Fat Bear! They are here, in chains, tied with a rope to the saddle of my horse!"

For an instant the uproar stilled. The shrill cries of the

145

Indians stopped. Joseph shouted, "Come and get them! Punish them as you will! But remember well the promise of Spotted Horse! The town is not to be attacked!"

The young Indians who had been around the fires on the hill came forward running. They surrounded Joseph's horse and went beyond to seize the three buffalo hunters and drag them toward the fires. The hunters looked up at Joseph as they were dragged past. Their expressions said they knew what was in store for them. Their eyes condemned him for surrendering them to be butchered by the Indians. Holloman yelled, "You dirty Judas son-of-abitch!"

It angered Joseph, whose conscience was troubled enough by what he had done. He stared Holloman straight in the eye. "Judas? I'm more one of them than I am one of you."

He turned his horse to ride away. He found himself blocked by half a dozen Indians. One he recognized. It was Badger, who had caused him so much trouble when he returned Fat Bear's body to his village for burial.

Badger spoke in the Cheyenne tongue, "Stay, brother, and help us kill the white murderers." His eyes were wicked, mocking, bright.

Joseph shook his head. "I brought them to you. That is as much as I will do."

Badger turned to those with him. "He is one of them. Let us kill him too."

Joseph yanked his gun from its holster at his side. He raised it, thumbing back the hammer as he did. But Badger had expected him to resist. He had a knife ready in his hand. With a swift movement he threw it, glinted in the firelight. It buried itself in Joseph's chest.

The pain was sudden and terrible. It was like a giant

146

fist, closing on Joseph's heart. But he had Badger in his sights. All he had to do was squeeze the trigger and Badger would be dead.

A look of triumph was in Badger's eyes, a look that Joseph suddenly understood. Badger was willing to die at Joseph's hand. He was willing to die to prevent the Cheyenne from going away without attacking and destroying the town of Indian Wells. He knew his own death would inflame them so that not even Spotted Horse could persuade them to leave peacefully.

Joseph eased the hammer down. His face twisted with the almost unbearable pain of the knife in his chest as he shoved his gun back into its holster. He touched heels to his horse's sides and rode straight through the half dozen Indians toward the town of Indian Wells.

For an instant there was silence behind him, silence from Badger and from those with him. Then Badger shouted with a terrible, balked fury, "Kill him! Kill him! Do not let him get away!"

Joseph dug spurs into his horse's sides. He leaned forward, clinging to the horse's mane with both his hands. The knife hilt still protruded from his chest. He dared not withdraw it, knowing if he did he would bleed to death before he could get back to Indian Wells.

Shots racketed behind. One bullet struck his horse in the rump, making him jump and shy so violently Joseph was almost unseated, making him run even faster than before. A second bullet struck Joseph in the thigh, entering and coursing the length of it, to shatter his right knee as it exited.

Joseph was hanging on now for his life, but his life was ebbing fast. No blood came from the knife wound, but he was bleeding internally from the artery it had punctured inside his chest. There was no strength in his

147

right leg and he began to sway helplessly from side to side, unable to brace himself with his right foot in the stirrup or even to steady himself with the pressure of his knees.

This way, he came into the town of Indian Wells. The hurt and terrified horse galloped down Main Street toward the jail. He shied violently when a man ran out of the Free State saloon and Joseph tumbled limply from the saddle to lie still and twisted in the dusty street.

Handy, a bandage around his head, heard the sound of the galloping horse. He went to the door of the jail, squinting because of the savage, throbbing pain inside his head.

He saw Joseph's horse in the light from the saloon and from the hotel across the street from it. He saw the horse shy so violently. He saw his son tumble from the saddle and lie still afterward.

He was running, then, with Bird Woman running like a deer behind. Handy reached Joseph a little ahead of her. The two knelt in the dust at Joseph's side.

It was dark, but there was enough light streaming from the open doors of the saloon to see that Joseph's eyes were open, to see as well the knife still protruding from his chest. Handy opened his mouth to say that what Joseph had done had been unnecessary, that he had earlier decided to surrender the prisoners.

He never spoke the words. Joseph had given his life to save his father from a compromise of his principles, from a violation of his oath. He would not now tell Joseph that what he had done had been a mistake.

Bird Woman was weeping, her body shaking helplessly with sobs. There were tears in tough old Pete Handy's eyes because he had seen the position of the

148

knife, had seen Joseph's shattered knee.

But in Joseph's face he saw a peace he had not seen in his son since Joseph had been a little boy. No more would Joseph have to live among people who hated him. No more would he be torn between two ways of life. Joseph's eyes closed and his chest was still.

There was a sudden, terrible fury in Pete Handy's heart. He slid his arms under Joseph and lifted him. Without looking at any of the townspeople, he carried his son up the street in the direction of their tiny house. Bird Woman followed, weeping, half a dozen feet behind.

At dawn, Pete Handy rode up Main Street and out of town, leading a horse to which a travois had been rigged. He spoke to no one and he did not look back.

On the travois was the body of Joseph. Behind the travois rode Bird Woman, her face pale and drawn, but with all the tears gone at last from her eyes and heart.

At the edge of town, in the middle of Box Elder Street, Pete Handy stopped his horse. He looked back for a moment at this town he had served so long and well.

Slowly and deliberately he unpinned his sheriff's star. He looked down at it a moment, lying in his callused hand. Then he dropped it in the street. It was not as if he was rejecting the sheriff's job. Instead it was as if he was simply returning something that no longer belonged to him. He turned his face toward the north, toward the village of Half Yellow Face, toward the life he had always loved but which he had rejected so that his son could claim his white heritage. The three horses plodded slowly out of town, raising a little plume of dust into the still autumn air.

Adam Colfax stared after them, his jaw tightly clenched, an unaccustomed shine in his narrowed eyes. He was thinking that he would write the story of Indian Wells. But it would not be the story of an Indian boy, wounded and displayed in chains in the window of the hardware store. It would not be the story of a town's barbarity. It would, instead, be the story of a man, a giant of a man. It would be the story of the sheriff of Cheyenne County, Kansas, in the year 1872.

We hope that you enjoyed reading this
Sagebrush Large Print Western.
If you would like to read more Sagebrush titles,
ask your librarian or contact the Publishers:

United States and Canada

Thomas T. Beeler, *Publisher*
Post Office Box 659
Hampton Falls, New Hampshire 03844-0659
(800) 818-7574

United Kingdom, Eire, and
the Republic of South Africa

Isis Publishing Ltd
7 Centremead
Osney Mead
Oxford OX2 0ES England
(01865) 250333

Australia and New Zealand

Bolinda Publishing Pty. Ltd.
17 Mohr Street
Tullamarine, 3043, Victoria, Australia
(016103) 9338 0666